THE MYSTICAL MURDERS OF YIN MARA

PRAISE FOR
MARSHALL RYAN MARESCA

Maresca offers something beyond the usual high fantasy fare, with a wealth of unique and well-rounded characters, a vivid setting, and complicatedly intertwined social issues that feel especially timely.

— PUBLISHERS WEEKLY

I love the complexity of Marshall Ryan Maresca's worldbuilding as the vast conspiracy underlying all the inner workings of Maradaine is emerging through the intertwining pieces coming together. It's nothing short of brilliant!

— FRESH FICTION

It's a story about morality, about sacrifice, about what people want from life. It's a fun story–there's quips, swordfights, chases through the streets. It's a compelling, convincing work of fantasy, and a worthy addition to the rich tapestry that is the works of Maradaine.

— SCI-FI AND FANTASY REVIEWS

ALSO BY
MARSHALL RYAN MARESCA

FROM ARTEMISIA BOOKS

The Mystical Murders of Yin Mara

Hultichia*

The Withered Boy*

FROM DAW BOOKS

Thorn of Dentonhill

Murder of Mages

Holver Alley Crew

Way of the Shield

The Alchemy of Chaos

An Import of Intrigue

Lady Henterman's Wardrobe

Shield of the People

The Imposters of Aventil

A Parliament of Bodies

The Fenmere Job

People of the City

The Velocity of Revolution

An Unintended Voyage

The Assassins of Consequence

The Quarrygate Gambit*

*-Forthcoming

THE MYSTICAL MURDERS OF YIN MARA

A MARADAINE SAGA STORY

MARSHALL RYAN MARESCA

Chronological Note

The Mystical Murders of Yin Mara begins at the end of the month of Soran, 1215, shortly after the events of *The Imposters of Aventil.*

SHARAIN
Ressinar
Maradaine
PATYMA RIVER
MARAT
Abernar
MARADAINE
TOREN
Delikan
SAURIYA
THALIN
Itasi
MARADAINE RIVER
Kyst
SAURIC
Telin
Greilmar
GRELLIN
KES
Maskill
FANTHIC
Opiska RIVER
NIRADO
Lake Opiska
Opiska
PERIAN
Oriem
Yin Mara
CHENEN
YINARA
STALAKAE
Birr
RESECHET CANAL
Lacanja
RESSET
Posam

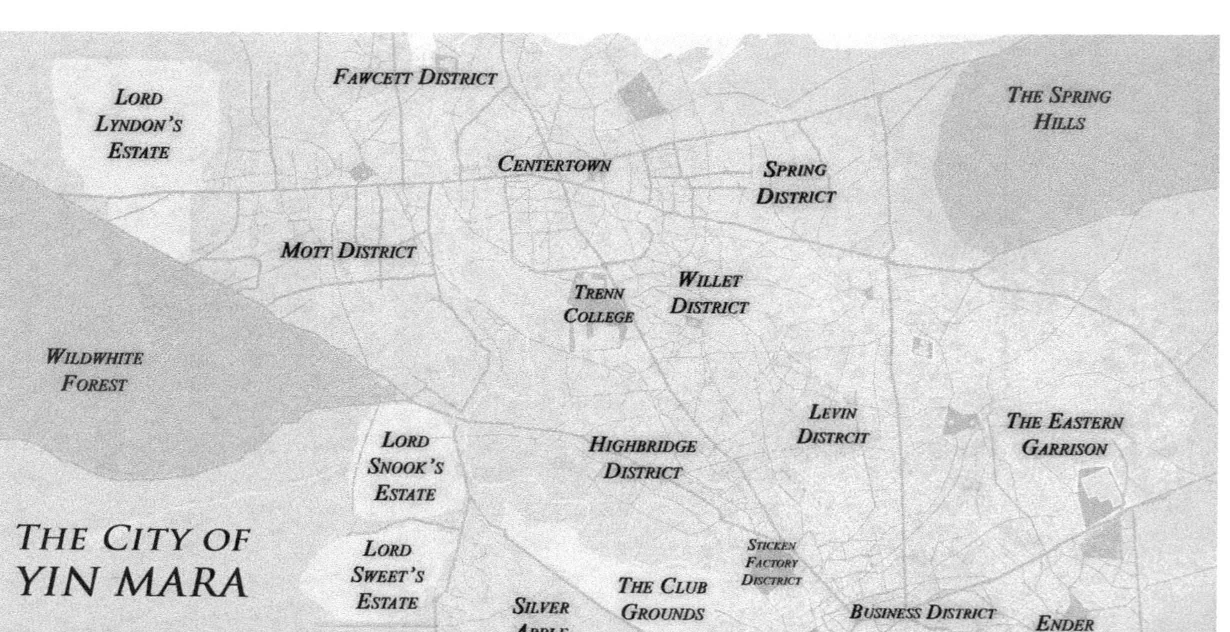

The City of Yin Mara
Lord Lyndon's Estate
Fawcett District
Centertown
Spring District
The Spring Hills
Mott District
Trenn College
Willet District
Wildwhite Forest
Levin Distrcit
The Eastern Garrison
Lord Snook's Estate
Highbridge District
Lord Sweet's Estate
Silver Apple
The Club Grounds
Sticken Factory Disctrict
Business District
Ender

CHAPTER ONE

A GENTLE KISS ON PHADRE GOLMIN'S forehead woke him from a doze he hadn't realized he had fallen into.

"Where are we?" he asked drowsily.

"Just outside Invell Valley, darling," the sweet voice of Jiarna Kay said in a low contralto whisper. "It's a town almost on the border between Sauriya and Yinara."

"'Almost' is imprecise for you, my dear," he said while rubbing his eyes.

"We're seven miles from the Sauriyal River," she said, leaning back in her carriage seat. "Presuming we leave punctually in the morning, we should cross the border before midday."

"That's a big presumption," Phadre said. Over the course of this caravan ride from Maradaine to Yin Mara, each morning's embarkment had been later and later. The schedule was to leave at eight bells each morning. Today they hadn't left until half past ten. "We were supposed to be on the riverbank today."

She gave him a bemused look. "You're cranky because I woke you up. Though saints know how you possibly sleep on this carriage."

"I just close my eyes and it happens."

"Lucky boy," she said, opening the carriage door and stepping out into the evening air.

"In many ways," he said, focusing on her. He was amazed how she managed to look so fresh and together after a day's travel in the carriage. Her long, black hair was braided, not a strand fraying or out of place, underneath her tilted schoolboy cap. Phadre knew if he wore such a thing, he would look foolish, but Jiarna had a way of making it look stylish. Her white blouse, violet vest and patterned skirt all still looked as crisp as if they had just come from the presser's iron.

She must have some brilliant scientific trick for achieving that, but she hadn't shared that with him. Despite their romance-filled summer, she still had her secrets. And that was part of what made him mad about her.

"You are probably famished," she said.

"Rather." He got out of the carriage, to see the crew of their Caldemane Company Cargo and Passenger Caravan working hard at unhitching the horses from the train of carriages and wagons. Mister Dreshin, the stubbled, leather-skinned underboss of the caravan, sauntered over to them. "Mister Golmin, ma'am," he said with a lift of his hat. "Trust your ride was comfortable today."

"He fell asleep again," Jiarna said.

"Then we kept as gentle as your mama's arms when you were swaddling," Dreshin said. "Though if you have any complaints, don't be shy about piping up, eh? Saints know your fellow passengers aren't."

Phadre was about to say something about leaving in a timely manner in the mornings, but a gentle kick at his ankle told him not to. Instead he said, "No problems that supper and a bed won't cure."

"Then you are in luck. The pension dining hall is ready for us, and your rooms are being prepared. I trust you both only need your top cases?"

"That's right," Jiarna said. "We'll leave you to your work."

As they went over to the pension, Phadre had to admit, despite the late mornings, the Caldemane Company ran an efficient business with impressive infrastructure. The passenger carriages were comfortable, and the drive crew were courteous and helpful. But the aspect that Phadre appreciated the most were the pensions. Just about every five miles on the highways throughout the western Archduchies, the Caldermane Company had built pensions with clean rooms, bountiful kitchens, and modern amenities with exacting standards. Phadre had to admit he was perplexed how these roadside facilities managed functioning water closets despite being several leagues away from any sizable city, but he was not complaining.

Carriage, meals and rooms were all included in their fare to Yin Mara.

Of course, the fare had cost a considerable number of crowns, a figure that made Phadre blush when he first heard it. Yet Trenn College was excited to bring both him and Jiarna onto their research faculty, to the point where they were offered sizable salaries and a travel stipend. With the college coffers backing them, there was no reason *not* to take the Caldermane Company carriages.

"Welcome to the Invell Valley Caldemane," a well-groomed valet said as they entered the pension. "I trust you are passengers of the caravan that just arrived." He held a manifest tightly in his hand.

"Phadre Golmin and Jiarna Kay," Jiarna said.

"Yes, of course," the valet said, looking through his papers. "Mister Golmin and *Miss* Kay. I have you in room 17— *together.*" He said that with as much disapproval as he could manage while maintaining a cheerful, professional demeanor. "Your room isn't ready yet, but you may avail yourself to the dining room, and by the time you've finished with supper, your bags should be in your room."

"That would be lovely," Jiarna said, not giving the man an inch in his condescension. "I presume the dining hall is this way?" She gestured to the archway to the right. The layout of the Caldemane pensions were nothing if not consistent.

"The rest of the passengers have already sat down," he said. "You two are the last."

"Thanks," Phadre said. "We'll get to dinner, and be expecting our room shortly thereafter."

"We will meet your expectations, Mister Golmin," the valet said, repeating the phrase the staff at every Caldemere pension would use.

They went into the dining hall to find the large table mostly filled up, with only two seats at the far end available. It meant they were, again, sitting with Mister Crenningsham.

"Our fault for being slow," Jiarna muttered.

"My fault for dozing off," Phadre said.

"It'll be fine," Jiarna said. "We've faced crazed alchemists and addled drug-dealers. Dinner with a boorish lout is pure simplicity."

"Besides," Phadre said, noting how Mister Crenningsham was focusing his crumb-ridden mustache in the direction of Missus Grindel. "Perhaps he won't notice us."

"That is especially wishful thinking, dear. Even for a mage."

Jiarna was immediately proved right once they sat down, in no small part to Missus Grindel trying to push Mister Crenningsham's attention their way. "Our young scholars!" she said exuberantly. "We were wondering when you might bother to join us all."

"Just taking our time," Jiarna said as she pulled the biscuits and butter out from Mister Crenningsham's domain and passed them over to Phadre. "My mother often said, better done right late than wrong in a rush."

"Well," Missus Grindel said with that tone in her voice that reminded Phadre of his Aunt Nerry, who was always annoyed with him. "I am not sure how one can exit a carriage and come to the table wrongly, but I imagine there must be a way." She glared over at Crenningsham, who was shoving biscuits into his mouth with ferocity. Phadre had noticed that Crenningsham had an appetite that would rival a mage's, but he hardly had a mage's skinny frame to match it.

Phadre took his own biscuits and butter, meticulously preparing them. He might be ravenous right now— as he was most times— but that was no call to surrender civility. "What else do we have tonight?"

"We are still in Thalin country," Jiarna said, taking one of the bowls from further down the table and serving herself. "So that means—"

"Mustard cream onions, crisped chicken, stewed beet greens," Phadre said. "I am familiar." The meals were, of course, locally prepared, and even with the Caldermane promise of quality, there was something to be said for variety. A traditional regional dinner lost its flair on the seventh or eighth day of it. Still, Phadre was so hungry he almost didn't care.

"Tomorrow," Crenningsham said between bites, food visible in his mouth as he spoke, "We'll be in Yinara— specifically in the Nirado region. You have Nirado food before?"

"No," Phadre said. "Though I suppose we're going to have to learn to like it." Yin Mara, their eventual destination, was the largest city in the Nirado region of the Archduchy of Yinara. Phadre had heard plenty about Yinaran food in general, but he suspected those things— grilled fish, oysters and crabs— were native to the coastal parts of Yinara, the city of Lacanja. Yin Mara was deep inland.

"Now, here's the thing you have to remember," Crenningsham said, wiping at his face. "You'll be on the Trenn College campus, right? Right on campus, or in a house adjacent to it?"

"I'm not sure," Phadre said.

"Regardless, same area. So, you're right in the middle of things, by Centertown and the Willet District. Not a bad neighborhood, mind you, but..."

Crenningsham had given them essentially the same lecture on where to go and not to go in Yin Mara at nearly every opportunity since the trip began. Phadre wondered if the man truly didn't realize he was telling them the same thing over and over again, or if he just liked hearing his own voice.

Missus Grindel seemed pleased, as he was no longer focused on her. She engaged in conversation with Lettie and Aister Canton, a wealthy couple who ran a cloth-and-textile business in Yin Mara. The Cantons had been pleasant enough to Phadre and

Jiarna, but they made it clear that they lived in a very different part of the city from the campus.

Most of the passengers were folk who lived in Yin Mara who had visited Maradaine for the summer. Phadre and Jiarna, moving to Yin Mara to further their studies at Trenn College as part of Professor Salarmin's special research group, were definitely an exception. Crenningsham was also an exception, as he worked for Remenieux Spice & Trading, traveling up and down eastern Druthal from Erien to Korifina. "I know the best places to eat, sleep and play in every city," the man had said many, many times.

Phadre had taken note of Crenningsham's advice on places to eat— the man clearly liked his food. That was critical information to Phadre. He didn't use to have the sort of appetite most mages were known for— but that had changed after the incident with Veranix's napranium rope and Cuse Jensett's numinic batteries. Never before had he channeled so much *numina* through his body, and while he mostly recovered from the experience, it had altered his relationship with magical energy. Now he was voracious all the time, as if a dam had been broken inside him.

Despite that, he had been raised to eat like a gentleman, and he would never change that habit, regardless of his hunger.

"It's looking to be a lovely evening," Jiarna said. "I think we should take a walk in the night air after dinner."

"Capital idea," Phadre said. "We've been cooped up in the carriage, our legs could stand to be reminded what they're good for."

"We shouldn't stray far from the road or sight of the pension," Phadre said. As much as Jiarna adored him, she sometimes bristled at his tendency to be a bit too staid and cautious.

"Bah," Jiarna told him. "I noticed a clearing through that thicket, and there's clearly an easy path to it. There's no risk." She led him over to the path.

"As you say," he said.

Even as they went through the trees, she could still hear the pension, especially the caravan bosses and drivers. They were, as usual, having a bit of a rowdy time around the stable house. Nothing too rough or coarse, of course— she had seen worse from college boys in social houses. It was an audible reminder that despite being out of sight, they were not too far from the rest of their fellow travelers. Should any trouble befall them— a situation Jiarna found highly unlikely — they were certainly close enough that a spirited cry would bring help running in moments.

"Onali has set already," Phadre said as they entered the crimson-tinged clearing. It was lit only with the light of Namali.

"Like I said, a lovely night." Something about an evening with a strong presence of Namali—just starting its waning gibbous, still nearly full— made her heart race and her blood rush. Perhaps it was fitting that outside of academic circles, Namali was called "The Blood Moon."

"Indeed," he said, staring at the sky. "You did bring a scope, yes? Look at Ghenix."

The bright orange wandering star was in the constellation of Hestru— the Hammer— tonight, as it had been for most of Soran and would continue to be halfway through Oscan. It was not the slowest of the wandering stars— that was Lemeschi, not visible right now in Peccicar— but it's movements through the stars were steady and deliberate.

All seven wandering stars had their motions charted and well documented, of course. Any scholar of the sciences could easily determine the current standing of all seven, as well as the phase of both moons, by consulting the High Collegiate Almanac.

Jiarna had long since memorized the patterns logged in the Almanac, so she knew where every wanderer was, and could name every visible constellation.

But seeing them was the wonder, especially out here away from Maradaine. This was the furthest from that city she had ever been, and out here without the bluster of urban life, there was nothing more magnificent than the wondrous beauty of the night sky.

All the mysteries it held, begging to be solved.

Celestial bodies, and their effects on magic and other mystical energies, was a small part of the work she and Phadre would be doing at Trenn College, studying with the infamous Professor Salarmin. She was giddy with the possibilities of what she could discover, especially surrounded by like minds, unique thinkers willing to examine the wide mysteries of magic and mysticism with scientific rigor.

"Where are you?" Phadre whispered.

"On Ghenix, perhaps," she said wistfully. "To us, it's just a speck of light, but do you think it's possible that it's just another world like our own? That possibly some young scientist is standing in a forest there, staring up at their sky, at us, and wondering what secrets our speck of light held?" In her mind— as fanciful and unscientific as this notion was— Ghenix was a lush and dense jungle, but the leaves on the trees were all orange instead of green.

"Can I join you there?" Phadre asked. She smiled and wrapped her arms around his neck.

"Anywhere and everywhere, darling."

As she moved in to kiss him, a scream pierced through the air.

JIARNA'S INSTINCT was to run toward the scream, and Phadre did the same, charging down the forest path back toward the pension. They matched pace, racing around to the back stables of the pension.

The scream stopped.

"Where is it?" Jiarna asked.

"It was a woman, I think," Phadre said. "That way." His hands were now charged with *numina*, crafting a nimbus of light around them. He went around the barn, and Jiarna followed right behind.

"Oh, dear saints," Phadre said, and he reached out to prevent Jiarna coming around to see it.

She saw it anyway, and she wasn't about to let him or anyone else spare her. But it was a horror.

The body— a man's body— was on the ground. He was dead, that was clear— beyond dead. Jiarna had seen bodies in her vivisection classes, witnessed carnage and violence in the drug riot on campus, but... she had never seen anything like this.

The skin was gray, and resembled a burned husk. Dry, and pulled taut, especially around his mouth, exposing his teeth and tongue. His fingers were desiccated to the point where they looked like bone, hands curled in twisted agony.

And his eyes—

His eyes were gone.

This man died horribly.

"Phadre," Jiarna said, her voice barely coming to her. "Did you see?"

"Exactly like this," he said, looking around. "No one else around. I didn't hear anyone run away."

"Did you… sense anything?"

He clearly gathered she meant magically. Phadre didn't have any particularly strong gifts for sensing numinic flow, but as a mage he had a fundamental connection to it.

"Nothing unusual," he said.

Jiarna reached into her pocket, despite her trembling hands, and took out her eyepiece— the lenses treated with dalmatium salts. Putting it to her eye, she could see the numinic flow all around her. Phadre was swirling with it, concentrating at his hands and head.

But around the body, nothing unique.

Phadre knelt down next to the body. "I would have sworn…" he said softly.

Two other people came running over. "We heard a scream," one of them said. They were both wearing uniforms of the pension, and Jiarna recognized one of them as the valet who checked them in. He wasn't the one speaking, though, as he had turned pale and sickly. He looked like he was going to throw up. The other man had the bearing of a manager, and looked like he was holding his wits together a bit better.

"We heard the same," Jiarna said. "We found… well, look."

"Jiarna," Phadre said. "I think…. I think it's Mister Dreshin."

She knelt down, taking the eyepiece out. The face had been turned into a dry husk, but as she looked closer, it was clear that the dead man was, indeed, the caravan underboss.

"Poor soul," the valet said. "You... you found him like this? Together?"

"Yes," Phadre said. "We were walking out in the clearing, and heard the scream..." Phadre paused for a moment, then shook his head. "We heard the scream and both came running over."

"We haven't touched him," Jiarna said.

"All right," the manager said. "Did you two see anyone else?"

"Not at all," Phadre said.

"Candling," the manager said to the valet, "Ride into the village to get the sheriff. I'll stand watch here."

"Ride? Alone?" Candling asked.

The manager sighed. "Or you stay with the body and I'll do it."

"I'll ride," Candling said, quickly darting off.

"The two of you are staying here? With the caravan?"

"Yes," Phadre said. "Under Golmin and Kay."

"All right, you should go back to your rooms. The Sheriff will probably have questions for you, but we've got this situation under control."

"Does the sheriff have an examinarian?" she asked the manager. "This body is not a typical death. You may need—"

"Miss," the manager said sharply. "Please go to your rooms. If your aid is needed, I'm sure the sheriff will be very interested in speaking with you. Until that happens, mind your own."

Jiarna wanted to protest, and struggled to fight that instinct. It wasn't their place to be a part of this, let the Sheriff handle things. Though there was something fascinating about this body. This mystery. There was no way— no way that she understood— that body could go from alive and hearty, to looking like a dried-up husk, in the space of an hour.

Which meant there was something to learn and discover here. That was an adventure.

But this was not the moment.

"Let's go to our room, dear," she told Phadre, pulling him along.

"I KNOW WHAT YOU'RE THINKING," he said once they got to their room.

"That the body is impossible?"

"Well, clearly not impossible," he said. "Since we both saw it."

"Right," she said. "Which means that whatever happened to it defies our understanding. So, there's no way the local sheriff is going to be able to understand it, either."

"Do you want to stay here to help them figure it out?" Phadre asked. "Abandon the caravan?"

She could tell he was legitimately asking her. If she said yes, he would gladly follow her, even though it would make them late for the start of their fellowship. She sat on the bed, taking off her boots. "No. Of course not."

"All right, then," he said. "Though one thing does strike me as very odd."

"What was that?"

"I would have sworn we heard a woman scream, and yet the victim was Mister Dreshin. But perhaps I was mistaken."

Perhaps he was. But that was another interesting piece of data. Everything about it was fascinating. It was a shame they would have to abandon this mystery to continue their journey to Yin Mara.

CHAPTER TWO

THE CARAVAN ARRIVED IN YIN MARA early in the afternoon several days later, bringing them up the main avenue of the Yin Mara Highway through the eastern outskirts to Centertown, the neighborhood with government offices and the largest shopping district. Phadre was quite ready for the journey to be done. Life on the road did not suit his temper, and this trip had ended any romantic notions he had once held about the idea.

Yin Mara was a much smaller city than Maradaine, far more spread out and low to the ground. As they came up the highway, they passed houses, stables, shops— but none of the high apartment tenements, factories or towers he was used to seeing as part of a city. Even as they approached the more bustling marketplaces of Centertown, no singular building stood out. A handful of brick buildings were a few stories tall, and up the hill to the west he could make out a red brick church tower, but it hardly screamed "city" to him.

Jiarna seemed to agree.

"Quaint and provincial," she said with a little sigh. "We were warned."

"It's charming," he said, hoping he'd make himself believe it.

"It has one of the finest libraries of science, one of the foremost experts on mysticism as a scientific study, and they're paying us to be here," she said. "I will be perfectly happy here."

Phadre let a smile come to his lips. "Then I'll be happy with you."

"Good," she said. "It is very quaint."

Phadre expected them to pull into a Caldermane city depot, much like the one they boarded the caravan on. Instead, the caravan— at least the passenger carriages— pulled into a wide square of impermanent stands and sale carts. The cargo wagons continued down the highway.

"Yin Mara High Markets," called the interim underboss, who took on Dreshin's work with a heavy heart. The mood on the ride for the last few days had been deeply subdued, which had probably impacted Phadre's own feelings about the trip. The death of Mister Dreshin, the image of his body, stayed with Phadre the whole ride. He wasn't sure if it had affected Jiarna the same way. But for the crew of the caravan, it was a heavy tragedy. "End of the journey."

Phadre and Jiarna disembarked from the carriage, finding their trunks unloaded and piled on the ground next to a vendor selling pennyhearts and swordpulps. "So what now?" Jiarna asked the underboss.

"What now is end of journey, ma'am," he said.

"Yes, but we're going to Trenn College campus," she said.

"You paid to get to Yin Mara. Welcome to it. The rest isn't our business."

"How are we—"

He walked away.

"Don't you dare—" Jiarna yelled after him.

"It's not worth it," Mister Crenningsham said, ambling over to them. "This is how they do it here, and you could yell in the face of Mister Caldermane himself, and it wouldn't matter."

"That's horrid, just to leave us here," Jiarna said. "We don't know this city. We don't even know how to get to campus from here."

"Oh, that's easy," Mister Crenningsham said. He pointed up the hill of the Yin Mara Highway. "That leads through Centertown until it splits into the Spring Turnpike and the Salt Road, and then the Great South Trenn Avenue crosses them both. Go right on South Trenn, it'll take you to it." He picked up his valise and started walking.

"Wait, Mister Crenningsham," Phadre called after him. "We should walk it?"

"Well, it's only about a mile up the hill, and then half a mile. It's not a big city, and you'll be walking all over Centertown in no time."

"But we have our trunks, equipment," Jiarna said.

Mister Crenningsham chuckled. "Of course, I forgot you two are moving here. A bit different for you."

Phadre had noticed that a carriage had arrived for Mister and Missus Canton, and they quickly loaded up and went off. Missus Grindel had her trunk, and she seemed to have employed a muscular young man to carry it for her as she went up toward Centertown.

"We might need to find our own muscular young man," he said, pointing Missus Grindel's arrangement to Jiarna.

"More like a small cadre of them," Jiarna said.

"I'm sorry I can't be more helpful, Miss Kay," Mister Crenningsham said. "About a quarter-mile up that way, before the bridge, there's a side road to the

Stone Plaza. I believe there's a livery stable and drivers for hire in there. You'll forgive me, but I'm overdue." He went off down the road.

Jiarna sighed. "The sensible plan is one of us walks to Stone Plaza while the other one guards our trunks and such here."

"I'm rather unfond of the sensible plan," Phadre said. "I neither care for abandoning you here, nor sitting idle while you venture forth to rescue us." On her raised eyebrow, he added, "Not that I doubt your capacity to handle either task. I would simply prefer not to get separated if it can be helped."

"And yet it can't," she said, kissing him on the cheek. "What's your preference? Stay here or go fetch the cart?"

"I'd do either as gladly as I could," he said. "Do you have a preference?"

She screwed her face in thought for a moment. "I think, logically, you are better suited for guarding our belongings. I'm more likely to elicit sympathy when hiring the cart and strong men to carry and load things."

"You think so?"

"I most definitely do." She pulled out a few coins from her purse and tossed it to him. "But it's best to limit my funds so my appearance is appropriately pathetic."

"Very logical," he said, putting her purse in his satchel.

"Methodical," she returned. "Always methodical." She kissed him on the cheek and walked off toward the hill.

On a whim, Phadre bought a sword-pulp book— a fanciful adventure of privateers against Poasians in the

Napolic islands— and sat on his trunk, reading as he waited. There was little else he could do.

After about a half an hour, Phadre became aware of a young man wandering around him and the pile of luggage. The young man was not of Druth stock, but Phadre couldn't quite identify what his heritage was. That, combined with the way the young man repeatedly seemed to be sizing up Phadre and his possessions, made Phadre more than a little nervous. He then chided himself for thinking such unjust things. The man's parentage was hardly cause to suspect him of untoward behavior or intent, yet Phadre's instinct brought him there.

That had come from father and grandmother, their fears and biases. Repetition had embedded those things into his own skull. Phadre reminded himself to do his best to root that out.

And the best way to do that was to confront his fear and bias directly.

"Sir," he called out. "Can I help you with something?"

The young man approached. 'Yes, right, sorry," he said quickly. "I'm just— you wouldn't be Phadre Golmin, from University of Maradaine?"

"I am," Phadre said cautiously. "And you?"

"Oh, excellent, many apologies," he said. He had a faint accent, which Phadre couldn't place. He extended his hand, "Acharriat Njien. I must have— yes, I see. I was wandering around you because I thought it might have been you, but yet… of course, you must have thought— yes, my apologies indeed."

"Hold up," Phadre said. "I'm not quite following."

"Yes, sorry, sorry," Acharriat said. "My thoughts are faster than my mouth. I came down to the market to meet you, but I was looking for two of you, and you were alone, so I didn't think you were you."

"Oh," Phadre said. "You're from the college?"

"Yes," Acharriat said. His hand was still extended. Phadre took it, finally, and shook vigorously.

"I should have known someone would have come down here to meet us. Did Professor Salarmin send you?"

"Yes, but, you're supposed to be with someone? Jiarna Kay? Did she not come on your caravan?"

"No, she did," Phadre said. "But she went in search of a wagon or such to bring our possessions to the campus."

Acharriat looked stricken. "I am so foolish! I should have come sooner, my friend, so you wouldn't have been waiting. We have a cart, waiting on the other side of the marketplace. That is where the caravans usually unload passengers, but today they did something else. What a terrible fault of mine this is."

"No, no, mate," Phadre said. "No harm, really." He didn't need this fellow beating himself up over such a minor oversight.

"I will rectify. I will run and tell Chren to bring the cart over here, and then run with even greater speed to find Miss Kay and explain my error." He dashed off before Phadre could even argue.

A few minutes later, a mulecart trundled over to him, driven by a young woman with a warm umber complexion. Definitely not of Druth stock, and Phadre's instinct was that she was Turjin, even though he had never met anyone of Turjin heritage.

"Hello," he called out. "Are you Chren?"

"That's me," she said. She also had an accent, but one that put Phadre in mind of southern Druthal, not any of the nations of Tyzania. Of course, he had no way of placing such accents. He quietly cursed to himself. Despite his education and living in the cosmopolitan city of Maradaine, his own experiences were quite limited and sheltered. He was the one that was quaint and provincial.

She hopped down from the cart. "And you're Phadre Golmin. Let's get your stuff loaded up." She grabbed one trunk, and despite her tiny frame, she easily hauled it over to the cart. Phadre quickly did the same with another trunk. There was no need to leave all the work to her; that would be unseemly.

"Forgive me," he said. "But what sort of name is 'Chren'?"

She sighed and nodded. "The kind that's easy for you to deal with." She hopped back up on the cart and pulled the trunks over to make more room for the rest of their possessions. "If you prefer, you can call me by my full name."

"Which is?"

"Chrenistinajovikam." That was almost definitely Turjin.

"What do you prefer I use?" he asked.

"'Chren' is absolutely fine," she said. "So, where's your lady?"

"She went off in search of a cart to hire while I waited here."

"You let her wander off in a strange city?" She said this with a certain sense of whimsy and mock horror, so Phadre knew he was being teased.

"One doesn't let Jiarna do anything," he said. "She'll do whatever she decides."

"I like her already," Chren said.

"I'm rather fond of her, myself," Phadre said, pulling another trunk up on the cart.

"You better be." Phadre looked up to see Jiarna

striding over, with Acharriat jogging beside her, getting winded to keep pace.

"I see you were found."

"Yes, this excitable fellow found me just as I was about to go into the livery," she said. "So it's good to know that the college did not abandon us to our own devices."

"Well, we were expecting you two today," Chren said, bending down from the cart to offer her hand to Jiarna. "Chrenistinajovikam. Good to finally meet you."

"And you!" Jiarna said, her eyes brightening. She leaped onto the cart and took Chren into an embrace. "Phadre, darling, this girl is a large part of why we're here!"

"I thought it was our notable talent and intelligence," he said.

"Well, yes, there is that," Chren said.

"But she and I have been writing each other for, what, two years now?" Jiarna said, looking at Chren. "She's been working with Professor Salarmin on mystical properties of crystals."

"Crystals, stones, gems. I like to call myself a magio-geologist."

Now Phadre felt especially silly. "You said your name was Chren. Jiarna, you always said your friend here was named 'Jovi'."

Chren stiffened for a moment. "That— that's not appropriate for you to call me."

"But you wrote—" Jiarna started.

"You, yes. Him, no. The men can call me Chrenistinajovikam in moments of formality, and for them, Chren is the acceptable name for them to use." There was something in Chren's demeanor that made it clear she would not field further questions on the matter. Phadre, not knowing more about Turjin naming conventions, decided to redirect things to end any further awkwardness. "So, Acharriat, I presume you are part of the Professor Salarmin's team, yes?"

Acharriat was leaning against the cart, still struggling to regain his breath. "Yes. Sorry, yes. I've got quite a few projects underway right now. Research, largely. I'm in charge of the library at Inchellian House."

Inchellian House. The hub of Professor Salarmin's academic establishment. He had assembled geniuses in magic and mystical theory from all over Druthal— all over the world, to look at Chren and Acharriat— and put them under one roof. This was where he and Jiarna would be living as they began their fellowship. Study, experimentation, teaching, and surrounded by like-minded people to bounce ideas off of.

It was a far cry from the four years of strange looks and raised eyebrows at the University of Maradaine. Of course, he had been supported, but he strongly suspected that the professors there— and especially his fellow students— never fully understood his work and theories.

No one had, truly, before Jiarna.

He knew she had faced far worse in the women's college. She baffled her faculty, and had to fight tooth and nail to get Professor Alimen to take her even remotely seriously.

To think, now the University of Maradaine was angry at their departure. But U of M's loss was definitely Trenn College's gain.

"Are we all loaded?" Phadre asked.

"Yes," Chren said. "Let's get you up to the house, and settled in. Then you can meet the professor and the rest of the team."

THE RIDE through the streets of Yin Mara to Inchellian House was a bit too hot for Jiarna's tastes. That was the main thing she was starting to realize about this move. Yes, it was the end of a particularly strident summer, but it was a muggy, dank sort of heat that was very unlike the Maradine summer. She also noticed that the flies seemed to be prolific— large, heavy insects that seemed to have a marked interest in burrowing into her hair. Perhaps that was a result of being on the mulecart, but she noticed flies diving at Jovi and Acharriat, who both gave the creatures little regard.

So maybe that was how it was in Yin Mara. She'd have to find a way to deal with that. Not accept it, like the locals, but solve it.

"Dearest," Phadre whispered to her. "Do you know why she's Jovi to you and Chren to me?"

"Not completely," Jiarna said. "It's something tedious about Turjin customs involving the interactions of men and women, though, and elements of their long form name are utilized differently."

"So she's from the Turjin Empire?"

Jovi had glossed over these points in some of her letters, but the details didn't matter at the moment. "Born there, but her mother fled some sort of atrocity and eventually ended up in Korifina. That's where she grew up." And fortunately so, Jiarna thought. She had put a little bit of study into the Turjin Empire when she had taken up the correspondence with Jovi, and what she had read horrified her. Women were apparently not allowed to be educated there. She couldn't imagine how a brilliant mind like Jovi's would have withered in such an environment.

Phadre spoke up to be heard by the others. "So how long have you been with Professor Salarmin?"

"Three years for me," Jovi said. "And you're on, what, five?"

"Four," Acharriat said. "I am sorry that I only would be allowed one more year here, and then I must pursue something beyond this fellowship. Perhaps my own professorship. And you, I have read some of your papers that you sent. I am quite intrigued by this Unseen Moon of yours."

"I still don't like that name," Jiarna said. "We should use an Old Kieran name."

"Bah," Phadre said. "The moons and fixed and wandering stars have Old Kieran names because everything was named by them two thousand years ago."

"Well, that depends on what part of the world you're in," Acharriat said. "Sorry, continue."

"My point is, if we find it and prove it's there—"

"It's there," Jiarna said. "The Winged Convergence is impossible unless some other thing is bending how we see the two moons in the sky."

Phadre gave her the look he always gave when she explained something he already knew.

"My point," he said again. "Is that this will be *ours* to name. I'm not about to give that to long dead Kierans."

"I agree with Phadre," Jovi said. She had turned down a road that was even more sparsely inhabited. The right side was a tree-lined walkway, that led past a park and a tiny lake. On the left side was a graveyard.

"Are we close to campus?" Jiarna asked. "I thought it was by Centertown."

"It's just past here," Jovi said, pointing down the

road. "The house isn't, strictly speaking, on campus, but right next to it."

"So are we in Aventil or Dentonhill?" Phadre asked.

Acharriat raised an eyebrow. "What does that mean?"

"Sorry," Phadre said. "The two neighborhoods by the U of M campus were… I don't quite want to say dangerous."

"A little dangerous," Jiarna said. "Well, one is dangerous, the other is more unwelcoming."

"Oh, no, nothing like that," Jovi said. "There isn't really a dangerous neighborhood in this city."

"What?" Phadre asked. "I mean… I find that a bit difficult to swallow."

"Well, we don't go over to the Fawcett District by the river, of course."

"Or Ender District," Acharriat said. "But that's on the south side, far out."

"Right," Jovi said. "Or anywhere near the factories or the garrison."

Jiarna had already studied a map of the city, so she understood what they were talking about. But understanding and experiencing were two different things. Even still, she doubted this city sported the sort of perils one frequently saw in the streets of Maradaine. Though it was clear that, at the very least, Jovi and Acharriat rarely ventured outside of the areas they had deemed as safe.

She chided herself for thinking unkindly of them for that. She had hardly expanded her horizons from the sequestered enclave of the University of Maradaine until adventure found its way to her. And they were a Turjin girl and a… whatever Acharriat was— in a city that was smaller and far less cosmopolitan than

Maradaine. She wondered if there even was a Little East or similar neighborhood here.

The cart pulled off the road, down the walkway of a sizable house that stood out from its neighbors. Most of the houses here were made from reddish-brown bricks, and this one kicked the eyes with its yellows and whites. All the windows and doorways were topped with arched gables, with patterns of alternating yellow and red brick. The same type of archway covered the walkway next to the house, creating a protected port for the mulecart. Several of the rooms on the top floor had balconies and turrets, and the front of the house had a wraparound portico with thin columns.

The house was glorious, and the idea of living here made any reservations Jiarna was feeling about Yin Mara melt away.

As the cart came to a stop under the port, three people came out the side door to greet them. Two of them were about the same age as Jovi and Acharriat, both of them far more traditionally Druth in appearance and complexion. The young woman, Jiarna thought, was almost a mirror image of herself, if she had no sense of style. The girl wore a coat and pullover that were far too large for her body, and her hair was a tangled mess that fell in her face. The young man, on the other hand, was blond and beautiful, in that perfect Social House Boy sort of way that Jiarna no longer found as appealing as she had a few years ago.

The third man was older, perhaps in his fourth decade, and he had the dusky complexion indicating Acserian or Imach heritage. His neatly groomed beard and tied-back long hair was dark black, salted with streaks of white. He could only be Professor Salarmin.

"Welcome, welcome," he said with wide smile and open arms. He clapped his hands together energetically. "So pleased that you arrived safely without incident."

"Safely, at least," Phadre said, dropping off the cart. "Phadre Golmin, sir. Pleasure to be here."

"Pleasure to have you, son," Professor Salarmin said, taking Phadre's arm warmly. "Was there incident for you? Nothing too troubling, I hope."

"One of the caravan crew was murdered," Jiarna said, coming up next to Phadre.

"Murder, really?" the mousy girl asked. She had an eastern Druth accent. From Vargox or Marikar, likely.

"Well, certainly dead, circumstances odd," Phadre said.

"Quite the bother," the pretty boy said. He reached out to Jiarna. "I'm Kennick, by the way."

"Jiarna Kay," she said.

"Yes, yes," Professor Salarmin said. "Let's deal with all the pleasantries. I am, as you've gathered, Professor Salarmin, and I'm thrilled that you are joining us here at Inchellian House as part of our team. A Mental Squadron, as I like to call it."

"We're both very happy to join you all," Jiarna said. Phadre started unloading the cart with Acharriat's help. Kennick stood on the side, more of his attention on her and the professor.

"You've met Chren and Acharriat, of course. And this is Kennick, of course. He's something of my lieutenant on this squadron, if you permit me the military metaphor."

"I've been here the longest," he said with a prideful smile. "Well, almost."

"And that's Geordi."

"Geordine Hollick," she said, keeping both of her hands firmly at her side. "I've taken the liberty of reading the letters and papers you sent to Professor

Salarmin and find them most intriguing." She said this almost as if it was one word, with no emotion or inflection.

"Should we bring the trunks and cases in, sir?" Acharriat asked. "Which rooms are we putting them in?"

"Let's worry about that in a bit," Professor Salarmin said. "Just put them in the entryway for now. I imagine our two new arrivals are famished, especially Mister Golmin."

"I certainly could eat," Phadre said.

"Then we should do our traditional welcome," Salarmin said. "Let's walk to the Friendly Hand."

CHAPTER THREE

PHADRE FOUND THE STROLL DOWN THE Great South Trenn Road quite pleasant as Professor Salarmin led their small party from the house back toward Centertown, past a lake on one side of the street and a graveyard on the other. Despite Jiarna's protests, the city wasn't some pastoral village; it certainly had a quaint charm he enjoyed. He wasn't sure which parts of those charms were because of its size, and how much were part of the local flavor here in the Nirado region of Yinara.

"So you're actually a mage?" Kennick asked as they walked.

"Do you need proof?" Phadre asked back. "I mean, yes, fully Lettered Mage, Lord Preston's Circle. I wouldn't put myself out to hire or anything like that, but I know what I'm doing."

"He's being modest," Jiarna said. "He's very talented."

"Talent through knowledge," Phadre said. "I don't exactly knock the walls down with raw power. Not like some folks I studied with at U of M."

"I've heard the Marys are the best for magic," Kennick said.

"They are very good at training people with raw ability," Professor Salarmin said. "I'm glad I snatched you two away, because I suspect they were counting on you two to beef up their theory program."

"I heard rumor that they were a little upset about that," Jiarna said, her voice trilling with joy. "Their loss, though."

"Your theories are really fascinating," Geordine said in a rapid mumble; so fast and quiet, Phadre barely heard it.

"Which ones are you…" Phadre started, but she had already started to walk faster, a few lengths ahead of the rest of the group.

"That's actually her being very friendly," Chren said. "It took weeks for her to warm up that much to me."

"If you say so," Phadre said.

They reached the plaza where Great South Trenn crossed the fork where the Grand Yin Mara Highway split into the Salt Road and the Spring Turnpike; a small park surrounded by shops and other businesses.

"That's the grocer we usually get supplies from," Acharriat said, pointing to one store. "First thing you need to know, Inchellian isn't a Social House. We don't have a staff, there's just the six of us. Well, seven with Lasilin, but don't count on him for anything."

"Who's Lasilin?" Phadre asked.

"So that means we do our shopping, our cooking, our cleaning, all together, all as a team," Acharriat said, barreling on as if Phadre hadn't asked a thing. "That's all of us, Kennick."

"I know," Kennick said.

"Which means you don't leave it to the ladies and the foreigners, hear?" Acharriat said. This was aimed more at Phadre.

"I lived in a home with plenty of chores," Phadre said. "I can pull my weight, especially with keeping tidy."

"He's quite good at being tidy," Jiarna said. "Which is good, because that's my failing."

"We balance each other well," Phadre added. "But this Lasilin…"

"There's the Friendly Hand," Professor Salarmin said. "It's always something of a tradition for us to come here when someone new comes along, or we have a particularly notable victory. But you might like it enough to come on your own, if that's what you wish."

The place stood alone in a patch of well-manicured grass on the far corner: a charming pub house of red brick with white trim and gabled roofs. Phadre couldn't imagine such a place in Maradaine— there would be no grass, and tenements jammed in on both sides. If it was in Dentonhill, there would be an *effitte* addicted transient laying in the doorway as well. The bright cheer of Yin Mara was already having an effect on his spirits.

So were the smells coming from the Friendly Hand.

They went in and were escorted to a long-benched table. "So what's your craving today?" asked a young blonde woman with a crooked-toothed smile.

"Sweet pigs all around," Salarmin said. "Tang and sour them, and also a bowl of salt tates for the table, and honey tangs for us all."

"You got it," the girl said with a wink.

"What are we having?" Phadre asked Jiarna in a low whisper.

"You were curious about Yin Mara cuisine," she said. "Looks like we're about to find out."

"You are indeed," Salarmin said. "I will tell you,

there were many schools in Druthal where I could have written my own way. RCM. Coanware. The Acoran Conservatory. They all wanted me. But Trenn College and Yin Mara had sweet pigs and sour cabbage and salt tates."

The server came back with iced drinks served in tall glasses.

"Iced? You use ice in drinks down here?" Jiarna asked, taking a sip of hers. "Oh, that's charming."

"It's practically a necessity," Kennick said. "Ice is probably the biggest import to this city. People always want it."

Phadre took a sip— it was cold, crisp, sweet and bubbly. Honey sweet, with a hint of mint and citrus. "How does it fizz?" he asked.

"I've read about that," Jiarna said. "Gassing beverages is all the rage in the south. Hasn't made its way to Maradaine."

"You mean something innovative didn't come from Maradaine?" Kennick asked, his tone a little mocking. "I thought that city was the jewel, the forefront of everything brilliant and modern in the world."

Phadre just put on a smile. "We have to let the rest of the world have a few victories," he said. "It's no fun, otherwise."

"Well said," Acharriat said. "Else why would you come here?"

"They come here because of sweet pigs and salt tates," Salarmin said exuberantly. He must have seen the server coming with plates stacked on her arm, laying them down in front of everyone. The "sweet pigs" that Professor Salarmin was raving about were sausage sandwiches, presumably pork, slathered with mustard and pickled cabbage.

Phadre remembered how the athletes from Trenn

college were derisively called "cabbage eaters" during the Grand Tournament. Now that made sense.

In the center of the table, the server put a large steaming bowl of boiled potatoes, but the potatoes were coated in sparkling crystal. Professor Salarmin grabbed one immediately, and then tossed it between his hands for a moment before biting into it. It was obviously too hot for his mouth, and he started hyperventilating to air it out.

"So good," he said, despite still having steaming potato in his mouth.

Jiarna gently touched Phadre on his leg, and then squeezed, as if to ask, "What have we gotten into?"

Phadre picked up one of the potatoes and blew on it, throwing just a hint of icy magic into his breath. Satisfied he had cooled it sufficiently, he popped it into his mouth. As soon as he did, it was clear what the sparkling crystal was— the potatoes were covered in a crust of salt.

Which explained the name "salt tates." Phadre sometimes wondered how he could be so brilliant about complicated matters but dim about something basic.

Still, they were quite tasty. He could clearly see the appeal.

"So," Jiarna said, trying her own food with a bit more care and decorum. "What can we expect for our responsibilities as part of the team?"

"Well, once we get you settled into your rooms—"

"Rooms?" Jiarna asked.

Salarmin laughed uncomfortably. "Well, I didn't want to presume any sort of arrangement the two of you might have. But it's best that you each have a room, at least formally speaking. Looks good on paper for the people who supply the money."

"Of course," Jiarna said.

"Mind you, I don't care what you do. All six of you could sleep naked in a huddle in the common room for all it matters, long as the work is done."

"No," Geordine said quickly.

"The work," Jiarna stressed.

"I presume it's researched based," Phadre said, taking a bite of his sweet pig. It was quite a good sausage, and while he didn't care for the cabbage part of it, the rest of it was quite enjoyable. He imagined that, in the future, he could order it without the cabbage. That touch seemed to be specifically the Professor's preference. Both Chren and Geordine were pushing their cabbage to the side.

"Research, yes," Salarmin said. "We're all exploring different facets of mysticism, and the two of you will be expected to find your own projects that cover unique ground. There will be other chores, of course. Maintaining the household, teaching first-year classes, that sort of thing."

"What will we be teaching?" Phadre asked.

"Oh, the sort of thing you can do in your sleep," the Professor said. "Basic science, basic magic theory. Nothing that will draw too much of your time from your research. Individually and with the group."

"So we all work together as well?"

"We each do our own projects," Kennick said. "But the idea is that our projects complement each other."

"Precisely," Professor Salarmin said. "And with that, hopefully, we will delve into the deeper connections that bind all of mysticism."

Another squeeze from Jiarna. But this one, he could tell, showed her pure excitement. This was what she had come for.

WHEN JIARNA first saw her room, the first thing that came to her mind was The Virgin Tower. She hated reading that book in her literature class— a class she only took to fulfill her base requirements for her Letters of Mastery— but it provided her the perfect comparison for this situation.

Her room was on the third floor of the house, but isolated from the rest of the third floor, so the only way to get to the room was by the spiral staircase, which led down to the floor with the rooms Jovi, Geordine and Acharriat stayed in. To get to Phadre's room, she would have to go all the way down to the ground floor, then across to the other side of the house, and back upstairs to the second floor. That itself wasn't a big problem.

But the spiral staircase leading to her room, alone in the tower, was the noisiest, creakiest set of stairs Jiarna had ever experienced in her life. Every single step groaned or cried out and it would be impossible to get to or leave her room without everyone else on this side of the house knowing it. Unless she went out the window and navigated the rickety catwalk that went directly to the observatory. However, a cursory examination of its disrepair made that an unsound option for casual use.

The noise of the stairs was a shame, because it really was a fantastic room, otherwise. The staircase came up in the center of the room, which was entirely round, with windows on all sides, giving her a view of the entire city in each direction. Her bed was deliciously comfortable, she had a grand desk and more bookshelves than she could currently fill.

The water closet was on the floor below her as well. That was less than ideal.

"This city is very sparse, isn't it?" Phadre said as he looked out of the window. "And I hope you enjoy the sun waking you up."

"That will be less than ideal, given how we'll be working at night," she said. "I might have to find another place to sleep after those long nights." She came over to him and kissed the back of his neck. "And curtains. Surely, curtains."

Jovi coughed from the stairwell. Jiarna had heard someone coming up, but hadn't said anything until they spoke. The door below didn't have a latch, and while she doubted anyone here would impose upon her privacy, she did find it slightly disquieting. "Do you have everything up here?"

"Mostly," she said, looking around. "The equipment trunk? Or did that go into Phadre's room?"

"I'm not sure," he said. "I should go settle my own things in, shouldn't I?"

"If you're set for now, the Professor wants you both in his office now," Jovi said.

"I'll still have plenty of unpacking to do," Jiarna said. "And saints almighty, I could use a bath and a change of clothing. This is still my traveling outfit, and I was not prepared for it to be this hot today."

"This isn't that hot," Jovi said.

"It's darn near sweltering," Phadre said. "Is this typical? This heat, this humidity? And the flies?"

"The flies are new this summer," Jovi said. "Kennick was talking about it a few months ago—they're some breed that comes out every six years, I think. They've been awful, but..." she shrugged. "We mixed up a chemical that keeps them away, but... I don't think it's a better solution."

"If that's life here, we'll adjust," Jiarna said, taking off her waistcoat and blouse, throwing them on the bed. "But I'm going to have to rethink my wardrobe in general, if this sort of heat is typical for the season." She went to her trunk as she undid the hasp on her trousers. She noted Jovi had turned around, covering her face. "Oh, what in holiness are you doing?"

"You're naked," Jovi said. "In front of me, and him."

"That's patently untrue," Jiarna said, as she was still in her chemise and skivs. "And nothing he hasn't seen many times. Please don't be foolish."

"But—"

She opened the trunk and pulled out one of her linen summer dresses. A bit too frivolous an outfit to meet with the Professor in, possibly. She held it up over her body, and looked to Phadre. "There's no mirror in here, what do you think?"

"I like it," he said.

"That doesn't help, because you like it all."

"True," he said. He waved his hand, and an image appeared in front of her— herself, holding up the dress, matching her movements.

"Oh, that is helpful," she said. Looking at herself, she said, "No, this won't do. Something a bit more studious."

"Do you have the U of M uniform?" Phadre said.

"Oh, darling, you can't be serious," she said, putting the dress on the bed. "That would be insulting. Though, Jovi— stop that!"

Jovi was almost prostrate on the floor. "I am intruding on your privacy, your shared intimacy—"

"Hardly," Jiarna said. "If I felt intrusion, I would have said so. Now, what are the colors of Trenn again? Yellow and green?"

"Yes," Jovi said.

"Perfect," Jiarna said, digging through her trunk.

She pulled out a light yellow blouse, a green cravat and matching cotton trousers. Not perfect for this heat, but tolerable. She put those on and inspected herself in Phadre's magical reflection. Quite acceptable. "I'm going to need new hats."

"Now?" Phadre asked.

"This will do for the moment, so no," she said. Phadre dissolved the reflected image. "Shall we?"

PHADRE FOLLOWED Jiarna and Chren down to the Professor's office, finding him waiting with Kennick and Geordine. All three of them looked a bit listless, with the Professor pacing about a grand slate board.

"Ah, finally," Professor Salarmin said as they came in. "I take it you are all settled into your rooms, ready to begin?"

"More or less," Jiarna said. "And quite eager to."

"Excellent," he said. "Let me go over our priorities. First, your obligations to the college. You will be expected to teach classes for my department. At the University of Maradaine, do they do a two-day class cycle?"

"Yes," Phadre said. "Each set of classes every other day, with holidays skipped."

"Sensible," Professor Salarmin said. "Not what we have here."

"Three-day cycle," Kennick said.

"Anyhow, both of you will take on lectures for basic mystical theory— first years and second years, mostly. Those are first day and second day for both of you. Jiarna will take the eight bells class, Phadre the eleven bells."

"In the morning?" Jiarna asked. He knew she did

not care for early rising, especially when she planned on making stellar observations.

"These are classes that need to be covered, and you two are the new ones."

"You get the short luck," Geordine said absently. She scribbled in her journal as this was going on, barely looking up.

"Now, Phadre, you're in Lord Preston's Circle, yes?"

"Yes, sir," Phadre said.

"I'm going to, I hate this term, but *lend* you out to the School of Magic here, to handle their demand for practical magic."

"I'm happy to help," Phadre said. "I don't know if I'm the most qualified for that."

"More qualified than most. And there are quite a few magical students here. You'll more function in an advisory role for them. Third days, you make yourself available in the office for tutorial all morning."

"And my third days?" Jiarna asked.

"Also office tutorial, but for our students. Now, that's obligation to the university. Next, you have obligation to the house."

"To the house?" Jiarna asked.

"Well, there's the seven of you here," he said. Kennick coughed at that. "I mean six. It's six of you now, right. You live together, you work together, you cooperate. Sharing duties of household— tidiness, meals, and so on."

Geordine held up a finger. "We all do every chore. I put together a plan, I assign tasks. Gripe at me."

"Don't mind doing my part," Phadre said.

"Good," the professor said. "Next, your obligations to me. We have special projects of research and study, of which I'm sure you're aware. Some of that is working toward the grand goal." He pointed to the slate board. "The Unified Mysticism Theory. All the elements of magic… the mystical, the natural, the unknown. We will determine how it all works, how it all connects. That is the legacy I want us to pursue."

"But we will have our own projects," Jiarna said. Phadre heard a touch of edge in her voice.

"You do, but bend that toward this goal. Which it should, from what I understand. You both are building further pieces of the puzzle."

"Of course we are," Phadre said.

"Now, we also have to occasionally impress the people who pay for all this."

"The college," Jiarna said. "That's why we're teaching, right?"

"The college couldn't even come close to paying for us," Kennick said.

"We have patrons among the local nobility," Professor Salarmin said. "We have special projects that are geared toward… impressing them."

"We play show pony for our supper," Geordine said.

"The point is, cooperate toward that end," the professor added. "It's usually not too much of an interference."

Phadre wasn't sure how he felt about that.

"But to our project?" he asked. "That is to add to your Unified Mysticism, and requires late night observation on our part."

"I'm aware," the professor said. "I trust you can manage."

"Certainly," Jiarna said.

Kennick popped up. "These two want to see the observatory," he said. "That is why you're here, no?"

"I won't pretend it wasn't part of the appeal," Jiarna said.

"It's our key interest, after all," Phadre said.

"It is, and it's my interest in the two of you," Professor Salarmin said, taking a pipe out of his desk and quickly lighting it. "I'm counting on you to craft better observation equipment, better ways to measure the magical. That's my hope here." He led them out the door, down the hallway to another set of spiral stairs. Phadre realized the room they were heading to was the twin of Jiarna's bedroom, the high, circular room on the top floor. In fact, when they arrived up the stairs, it was quite identical in form, though nothing like it in contents.

There was a grand lenscope in the center of the room, larger than any Phadre had seen in his life. The rest of the room was occupied with desks, slateboards and other small pieces of equipment.

"Quite the beauty, no?" Salarmin asked. "Third largest in Druthal. And I'm anxious to see how it will work with your numinic camera."

"But the roof," Jiarna said, looking at the metal dome that would make using the giant lenscope impossible.

"I'll show you," Kennick said, walking over to a metal wheel on the wall. He started to turn it— hard, heavy cranks— and the dome of the roof opened up to the clear, sunlit sky.

"Amazing," Jiarna said, coming over to Phadre.

"Amazing, indeed," Professor Salarmin said, rubbing his hands together. "So let's get to it: plenty of work to do."

DAYS BECAME a routine in the household, as Phadre spent his mornings teaching the first-level magical theory classes, and his afternoons researching with Geordine or Achariatt, and his evenings working in the observatory with Jiarna. Where he would sleep— his room, Jiarna's or the observatory— on any given night would be changeable.

Jiarna was right on one point, hers was the better room, but he did always feel odd going up those stairs to stay up there. Though after a few nights, neither of them cared, and they knew that none of the rest of the housemates did either. Then they got in the habit of staying in the observatory until they fell asleep in there. That wasn't particularly good for their backs, but Phadre didn't mind, and Jiarna didn't seem to either.

After two weeks, the rhythm of the house was very beneficial for Phadre. He would have some idea about one of his stellar observations or concept of magical theory, and he would bring it up at breakfast, and in the afternoon someone else would come to him with an expansion of the idea or a piece of research that furthered his thoughts. It was incredible to be in an environment where so many people were at the same level as he was. He hadn't experienced that ever before, until meeting Jiarna. Now he was in a house full of like-minded people

One night, three weeks later, Jiarna had turned in early— her morning classes were demanding— but Phadre was too excited about getting more information in the observatory, and spent an hour alone taking readings from his meters and setting new plates in the numinic camera. It was good work, and once the plates were in position, he decided to slip to the kitchen to grab a quick bite of whatever was left in the icebox.

He had taken a plate of cold sausages and cheese out when he saw a wild-haired man in his skivvies.

"Oh, you've got the cheese," the man said, quite calmly.

"I do," Phadre said. "I'm sorry, and you are?"

"Hungry for cheese, all right," the nearly naked man said. He came over and took a piece off the plate. "You know if there's bread left?"

"Bread… left?"

"I'll look on my own," the man said. He went to a cabinet and began searching through it.

"Can I help you?" Phadre asked, trying to put enough edge in his voice to give the question a hint of threat.

"No, I know what I need," the man said, taking out a jar of mustard and another of pickles. He proceeded to put some on a plate, then a hunk of bread out of the breadbox.

Phadre found himself at an impasse. He definitely felt that he should take some steps to deal with this interloper, who surely was an intruder in the house. But at the same time, the man had such a casual ease and comfort in the kitchen, that Phadre felt as if he himself were the intruder.

"Who are you?" Phadre asked.

"Next time you go for dry goods, make sure to get more mustard." He took some more cheese and one of the sausages from Phadre's plate and put it on his own. Phadre realized he had been standing still in the middle of the kitchen the entire encounter, just holding the plate.

"Next time I— what?"

"Oh, and I think you're not taking into account your own numinic flow when you're taking readings in the observatory." He pulled a journal out of his skivs and handed it to Phadre. It was disturbingly moist. "Those are my own magic-null readings, the comparison should give you a baseline to calibrate for your own presence."

He wandered off down the dark hallway, while Phadre stood dumbstruck, plate in one hand, sweaty journal in the other. His appetite had left him, and he decided that he was possibly far more tired than he realized. Putting the plate back in the icebox, he blew out the lamps and went to bed.

He woke in the morning, spotting the journal on his bedstand as soon as he opened his eyes. Tangible evidence that he hadn't suffered a waking nightmare of some sort. The man in his skivs was real. He quickly dressed and went to the kitchen, where the rest of the group was already eating breakfast, including Jiarna. She was sipping her tea while reading the morning newssheet, which was a bit unusual for her.

"I had the strangest encounter last night—" Phadre started, holding up the journal. Before he could continue, Jiarna was on her feet.

"You won't believe this," she said. "Missus Grindel was found dead in the street last night!"

"Who's Missus Grindel?" Acharriat asked.

"She—" Phadre paused, unsure how take this news, though it seemed to overpower his own story for the moment. "She was on our caravan from Maradaine. And, dear, that is a tragedy."

"It is, but look at how she died!" Jiarna said, her voice more excited than horrified. She shoved the newssheet into his hands.

The article in question had a charcoal sketch accompanying, showing the grotesque scene the article described. The body was a dried-up husk of skin and bones, with no eyes. Just like—

"Just like Mister Dreshin!" Jiarna said.

"What does that mean?" Phadre asked.

"It means that this is a mystery we need to solve."

CHAPTER FOUR

T HEY HAD TO WAIT UNTIL THE afternoon to go to the stationhouse, after handling their responsibilities of teaching for the day. For efficiency, Jiarna said they should meet at the stationhouse after their classes, which meant Phadre was waiting outside for half an hour before Jiarna showed up. It gave him some time to look through the strange notebook of the sweaty, undressed man. While the handwriting was erratic, the data seemed to be well-presented and possibly valuable.

He needed to ask more questions about that man, or at least talk to Jiarna about it. He would presume it would be of extreme interest to her, were it not for the news of this body taking precedence.

"My apologies," she said when she came racing up to him, sitting on the decorative wrought-iron bench outside the stationhouse. Phadre had learned this about Yin Mara: they made the effort to make functional things also look pretty. The area outside the stationhouse was a festive floral garden, a very pleasant place to wait and read, and not at all putting Phadre in mind of a constabulary house.

"It's quite fine, though—" he started.

She held up a newsprint wrapped bundle. "Sweet pigs, no cabbage."

"You are quite thoughtful," he said. He had missed lunch to come here, and thus was more than a little peckish.

"I'm nothing if not aware of your body," she said. "Let's be about things."

Phadre dug into the sweet pig— with no cabbage it was, in fact, quite to his liking— as they went inside. The front office of the constabulary house was a quiet, open room where one lone woman— in some elder years— went through files with one hand while lazily fanning herself with a paper fan with the other.

"Pardon," Jiarna said. "We were wondering if we could speak to an inspector?"

The woman looked up slowly. "Was there a particular inspector you needed to speak to?" she asked in a soft drawl. "Or did you have a general report of a criminal act? That doesn't need to go to the inspector, after all."

"A specific inspector, I would think," Jiarna said.

"Because it's best to have one of the regulars go over the particulars of a crime before bothering any of the inspectors," the woman said. "I don't want to be wasting any time."

"We're here about the death of a Missus Grindel," Phadre said.

"Whichever Inspector is handling that investigation, we'd like a word," Jiarna added.

"I'm not familiar with that one," the old woman said. "Why does it concern you? Are you kin to her?"

"No, nothing like that," Phadre said.

"We saw in the paper her death had very unusual circumstances," Jiarna said. "The condition of the body was unique? Her eyes gone; her body desiccated?"

"Body what?"

"Dried up," Jiarna said, her voice taking an edge of annoyance. "Like an old apple."

"Oh, saints preserve," the old woman said. "I don't know of anything like that being investigated."

"It was in the paper," Jiarna said, taking out the newsprint and putting it on the woman's desk.

"Oh mercy upon us," the old woman said. "For them to print such a horrible image. It's a disgrace, it is."

"Is there an inspector looking into this?" Phadre asked. "We might have relevant information."

"Saints above, saints above," the old woman said. "You are both too filled with fire for me. Go down that hallway and talk to Inspector Stendall. He deals with any investigations involving people dying."

"Thank you," Phadre said. "Shall we?" he asked Jiarna.

She marched ahead of him down the hallway, muttering the whole way. "Absolutely ridiculous this city, only one inspector to deal with a murder."

"My love," Phadre said. "Before we go in, we should compose ourselves a bit."

She stopped, looked at him, then pulled a kerchief out of her pocket. "Yes, you've got a bit of mustard in the corner of your lip." She dabbed at it and put the kerchief away. "Much better. And I should focus on presenting my information in a cool and rational manner. We are people of science, and we should not minimize what we bring here by lacing it with anger."

Phadre had thought as much but knew it would be better if she took a moment to get there herself.

"I see the plaque for his office door there," Phadre said. He offered his arm to her. "Shall we?"

JIARNA KNOCKED, out of courtesy, and when there was no immediate response, knocked again with more fervor. She was about to knock a third time when the door swung open. A constabulary officer, she presumed, glowered at her. She presumed because he seemed to be in something like a uniform— the colors were not the green and red of Maradaine, but blue with gold trim— and the uniform itself, with its waistcoat and matching cravat, were very like the style of gentleman's suit that was in fashion in Yin Mara. But he did have a brass badge over his heart, with his name and title.

"Inspector Stendall," she said. "I apologize for any disturbance."

"What are you pounding on my door for, girl?" he asked. He squinted at Phadre for a moment. "You're probably in the wrong place, if you want to report a pickpocket or such."

"Nothing of the sort," Jiarna said. "We're here because we noticed in the paper the reports of the death of one Missus Grindel. We were told you're handling it."

"Grindel," he said, in a tone that made it sound like he wasn't sure which death that was.

"Have you had many unexplainable bodies turn up in recent weeks?" Jiarna asked. "I was under the impression that her death— the eyeless, desiccated corpse of a woman who was vibrant and healthy mere days ago— was remarkable enough to stick in the memory. But if this sort of thing is commonplace here, I apologize for my error."

"No, of course not," Stendall said, scowling at her

again. "I knew which one you meant, but why do you have any interest in it?"

"Missus Grindel was a passenger on the same caravan we came to town on," Jiarna said, indicating herself and Phadre. "That was nearly three weeks ago."

"You knew her?"

"We met her," Jiarna said. "But we hadn't seen her since the trip."

"Again, why do you have any interest in this?"

"Her death, at least as how it was described—"

"Listen," Stendall said, holding up his hand in front of her. "The newssheet was being very irresponsible, and I want to apologize for them printing that drawing. That should not have gone out to the general public. I've made it clear that they shouldn't be trying to shock and horrify—"

"I'm not shocked," Jiarna said. "Inspector, I'm not here out of some sense of impropriety. You have a dead woman—"

"It's shocking," Stendall said firmly. "And the newssheet people got there before we controlled the scene. I assure you, that won't happen again."

"The story, or a death like that?" Phadre asked. "Because unless you've caught the person responsible, you cannot assure the latter."

"Person responsible?"

"You can't see that as a natural death," Jiarna said.

"No, very much not," Inspector Stendall said. "But there's nothing to investigate. There's no *murder* here, if that's what you mean."

"I disagree," Jiarna said.

"Based on?"

"On the fact that there was an identical death on our journey down here," Jiarna said. "We saw that body with our own eyes."

"Where was this?" Stendall asked.

"At the Caldemane pension in Invell Valley," Jiarna said. "The victim was an employee of the Caldemane Caravan company. We were told the local sheriff would be handling matters, though we were not asked any questions by that office."

"We did have to leave the next morning, of course," Phadre said.

"This is noteworthy, thank you," Stendall said. "I appreciate the information."

Jiarna wasn't going to be so quickly dismissed. "Given the odd nature of the deaths— both of them— surely you suspect that magic or other mystical forces are involved."

"Other mystical forces?" he asked. "That sounds like the sew— mess you hear in country tales."

"Perhaps," Jiarna said. "But so does a body that looks like that."

Stendall frowned in concentration for a moment. "I suppose that's not untrue. Not sure what to make of that, but I'll reach out to Invell Valley and see what can be gleaned. Thank you for this." He made to shut the door.

"Sir," Jiarna said. "If there is magic or something of that nature at play here, we could be of use."

"Of use?"

"We're lettered masters in the sciences," Phadre said. "Both with expertise in magical arts."

"You're mages?"

"He is," Jiarna said. "I'm a scientist."

"We have an examinarian, children," he said. "But I'll keep that in mind."

He shut the door and latched it.

"We tried?" Phadre offered.

"We did," Jiarna said. "But I don't like letting the

mystery of it go, especially since it is no longer an isolated incident."

"I know," he said. "But we should get back to the house. It's not like there isn't plenty for us to do."

The made their way out, but not before Jiarna stopped at the officious woman's desk. "If the Inspector has further need of our services, we can be found at the Inchellian House on campus. It's Jiarna Kay and Phadre Golmin." When the woman just stared at her, Jiarna pressed. "Write it down. I feel he may need it."

THE HOUSE WAS abuzz with activity when they returned from the stationhouse, especially in the kitchen. Jovi and Acharriat were cooking frantically, generating scents that Jiarna couldn't put a name to. Geordine was preparing the table in the large dining room— a room that was mostly only used to store books overflowing from the library— while Kennick was sketching out diagrams on a large slate board.

"What's going on?" Phadre asked as they came in.

"Where have you two been?" Kennick snapped. "Do you know what's going on?"

"Not remotely," Jiarna said.

"We've got the Professor coming in an hour with the aides for Lords Snook, Lyndon and Sweet, so we need to have a stunning dinner ready, the dining room set and our proposals ready."

"Proposals?" Phadre asked.

"You do understand how we're funded?" Geordine shouted from the dining room. "The three earls of Yin Mara give generously to the house, but in exchange they want to be dazzled."

"Dazzled?" Phadre asked.

"Saints, you two!" Geordine said. "One of you help them in the kitchen, the other clear out these books!"

Jiarna exchanged glances with Phadre. She knew what she preferred of that arrangement, and hoped he felt the same way.

"I'll go to the kitchen," he said quickly.

Smart lad.

"Does it matter where the books go?" she asked Geordine. "Or is it mostly just 'not here'?"

"Not here is most important. And not the sitting room or the front parlor. Basically, anywhere the lords' people will come through. Everything else can be a disaster."

Jiarna noticed that Geordine was setting the table masterfully, despite the fact that she was doing it at a ridiculous speed. The young woman ran around the table, putting each utensil perfectly in place. It was something of a marvel.

"Stop gawking," Geordine said. "Just get the floor clear."

Jiarna hauled out piles of books, from mathematical treatises to personal journals, books in several languages on every topic. She had to resist the urge to thumb through them all, as time was of the essence, apparently.

Once she had the books out, she helped Geordine pull out the chairs, and together they quickly mopped the wooden floor with a vinegar solution, followed by a floral oil of Geordine's own creation.

"Instead of begging for funding, we should just sell this," Jiarna said, sniffing at the bottle.

"You think I didn't already run the numbers on that?" Geordine asked. "It's not tenable to raise the right flowers in the mass quantities necessary, not in this climate. In order to pull it off, you'd have to first raise capital on the market exchange in a way that would artificially inflate the sale price of the flowers and that would eventually ruin most of the investors. It's more work than I have time for."

"And… it's wrong to ruin your investors, yes?" Jiarna asked.

"I suppose there's that as well," Geordine said. "But mostly it's about the time. Though I suppose one could use cheaper florals to create a product that most people wouldn't have the sense to recognize as inferior." She furrowed her brow for a moment. "Though, no, still don't have the time for that."

Kennick came into the dining room, hauling the slateboards. "We ready in here?"

"Of course," Geordine said.

"Good, because—"

The front door opened, and Professor Salarmin strolled into the house with three finely dressed people.

"Should we change?" Jiarna whispered to Kennick. She was wearing the wool skirt and chalk-stained blouse that she had taught in this morning. Of course, Kennick and Geordine were dressed similarly.

"No, no," Kennick said. "Part of the facade we want to present. Impeccable house, but simple folks doing the scientific work."

Jiarna would have preferred to look a little stylish to match the three who came in with the Professor Salarmin, but she yielded to their experience in this matter.

"Ah, excellent," Salarmin said as he approached. "You all know Mister Mallin and Miss Hollick, but may I present Miss Jiarna Kay, formerly of the University of Maradaine."

"Yes, of course," the one woman in the trio said.

"You are the mage, right?"

"No," Jiarna said. "That's Phadre Golmin. I came down here with him."

The woman's face fell. "Oh, yes. And where is Mister Golmin?"

"He's in the kitchen with Chren and Acharriat," Kennick said.

"Really?" Professor Salarmin asked with a strained voice. "That's a surprising choice."

"It's what he preferred," Jiarna said.

Geordine went to the kitchen door and whistled to the others. Phadre came out, looking handsome and chipper, while Jovi and Acharriat both seemed a bit harried, but still with broad smiles.

"Hello, hello," Phadre said. "I take it these are our esteemed guests?"

"This is Phadre Golmin," Professor Salarmin said.

"And you've been cooking?" one of the new men asked.

"Helping them, they've been the real stars in there."

"He's being modest," Acharriat said. "He used his magic to facilitate the whole process immensely."

"Really?" the woman asked. "That is fascinating." She took Phadre's arm and led him to the table.

"Are we ready?" the third man asked. "Or are we waiting for Mister Kaiten?"

All the rest of the group seemed to take a collective breath, looking awkwardly to the floor.

"Mister Kaiten is no longer participating in this group," Professor Salarmin said. "Let's not dwell on that. Instead, we should sit and discuss the future. Jiarna, help bring the food out, won't you?"

The others all went and took their place at the table, leaving Jiarna alone in the space between the dining room and the kitchen.

CHAPTER FIVE

I N THE DAYS SINCE THE DINNER, Jiarna had been angry, and Phadre decided the best course of action was to give her space to feel that anger. She buried herself into the work, especially since the Professor had made it very clear the priority for the following weeks was to work on the two projects that had most interested the noble patrons: the numinic battery and the psychic compass. Those had been pitches that had come from Kennick and Chren, which meant they were taking the lead on the work, but both of them were planning on leaning hard on Jiarna.

That had not been what had made her angry, of course. She relished the work, as always. If anything, she would focus her anger into the work, going deep into research and development to the point where Phadre hadn't seen her in the observatory for days.

What had angered her was after the dinner, once the patrons' representatives left, Professor Salarmin had strongly admonished her in front of the group.

"Where were you this afternoon?" he had shouted at her.

"Phadre and I went to the constabulary station," she said.

He briefly cooled his temper. "Oh, I'm sorry. Had you been robbed or assaulted? I didn't know. You need to let me know about these things, Miss Kay."

"No, nothing like that," she said.

"Then what?" he asked.

"Someone from our caravan was found dead, in mysterious circumstances," she said. "We thought we might have insight to help the constables."

"It was undoubtedly the right course," Phadre had said quickly. "We had further information the inspector did not have."

"That's not my concern," the Professor said, his curt tone returning. "We're here to unlock mysteries of the magical world, and we do what we must to fund that, but we cannot be losing our focus to… assist the constabulary solve their crimes! I'm deeply disappointed in you, Miss Kay."

"We both went," Phadre said. "And I—"

"I'm not interested in further conversation. You all know what needs to be done, I suggest you get to it."

That had been the last they had seen of the professor for several days. Jiarna had settled to work, focused on her schedule, but she was definitely angry.

After six days, Phadre went to her room with cheese, bread and a bottle of wine. "Peace offering?"

She looked up from the journal she was reading. "Are we at war?"

"Perhaps not us," he said. "But I think you are upset, and I'd rather be part of the solution than the problem."

She got up from her bed and kissed him. "Appreciated." She took the bottle and went over to her desk, taking out a screw tool. "I'm sorry, I— yes."

"The professor was deeply unfair to you the other night," Phadre said.

"Thank you for saying that," she said. She opened the wine and poured some out for herself. "Took you a bit long, but it's appreciated."

"Sorry for that," he said. "I'm still a bit new at... this."

"Define 'this'," she said, sipping at her wine. He almost thought it was a trap, but he had some sense of how her mind worked.

"Being in a romance," he said. "As well as our living in this situation, our duties to the university and the professor."

"Is it a problem?"

"It's a challenge," he said. "Especially the full new situation here. But one I relish. Especially with you to face it with."

"I was..." she paused for a moment, and took another sip. "I was dismissed quite a lot at the University. Often by professors who didn't even understand what I was working on. But I never felt... diminished by them quite like this."

"You are not diminished," he said.

"I am here," she said.

"You and I—" he started, not entirely sure how to put this. "I know that I, for quite a large portion of my life, was often the smartest person in the room. Until I met you, and then you were."

"Phadre—"

"I mean it," he said. "But here? In this house? We are in a very different situation. I mean, all of them are on our level. Or higher. Blazes, I'm pretty sure that fellow in his skivs puts me completely to shame."

"The who now?"

"Did I not mention him?" Phadre asked. "It happened the night before we read about the body, and, well, in the excitement of things I never had the opportunity to bring him up with you again."

"A fellow in his skivs?" She sat on the bed, nibbling on the bread. "Please explain."

Phadre told the story of the man, his journal, and the rather astounding observations within that. "I did try to bring him up with both Kennick and Acharriat. On more than one occasion."

"And what did they say?"

"Nothing. They would immediately change the topic or leave the room. I then tested the theory with Geordine and found a similar reaction. I can only conclude that they all know exactly who he is, but are compelled not to talk of him for one reason or another."

"Mister Kaiten!" Jiarna exclaimed.

"Who?"

"You were in the kitchen, and one of the aides asked about Mister Kaiten, and the Professor's reaction was very interesting. 'He is no longer participating in the group.'"

"Well, clearly, he's not part of the group."

"Yes, but… not 'no longer with us' or 'isn't here anymore' or 'has left the group' or anything like that."

"So what are they hiding? Who is he?"

She jumped off the bed. "Come," she said, taking his hand. She dragged him down the stairs to Chren's door. Jiarna did not knock at all, simply charged in, taking him with her. Chren was on her bed, and on the sight of the two of them, squealed and dove under the covers.

"Jovi, stop that," Jiarna said.

"But he saw me in my *njarki*," she said.

"As did I, and you're covered neck to ankle, beyond

the demands of propriety in every part of this country. We need your help."

"It's very inappropriate," Chren said.

"I could leave—" Phadre offered.

"No, I will not tolerate such absurdity. Especially the absurdity regarding Mister Kaiten."

Chren lifted the blankets enough to stick her head out. "What?"

"You heard me," Jiarna said. "There is someone named Mister Kaiten who was part of this team, and while he is not part of it now, he is still, apparently, in this household. Everyone has been needlessly secretive to the detriment of Phadre and myself, so I do not care if it makes you uncomfortable. Tell us who this fellow is."

"And why he wanders at night in his skivs," Phadre added.

"What?" Chren asked. She lowered her voice to a horrified whisper. "You saw him? Was he… all right?"

"I mean," Phadre started, not sure how to answer that. "He was a fellow in his skivs, wandering through the kitchen. A bit odd. Took my cheese. But he also had made observations and notes in the journal he gave me that were, well, quite astute. Who is he?"

"Laslin Kaiten. He was the most brilliant one here," Chren said. "I mean, astounding, how his mind worked. And the Professor pushed him, drove him. Then he worked on something up in your observatory — something to do with telepathy, I never fully understood it, none of us did— and it went wrong. So wrong. He was broken, unable to form sentences for months. Then he recovered enough to talk, but… never was the same. He holed himself in the basement three months ago, but… I haven't seen him since. No one has, except the Professor, who told us to let him be and forget about him."

Jiarna shook her head. "That is very wrong. Such a thing, it shouldn't have been kept from us."

"I'm sorry," Chren said. "I shouldn't have. I know."

"Well, now we know," Phadre said. "And then—"

Geordine bounded into the room. "Hey, you two…"

"Must everyone come in my room?" Chren shouted.

"Sorry," Geordine said. "But, hey, there's an Inspector fellow at the door looking for the two of you."

"Us?" Phadre asked.

"Yeah," she said. "He said there's a third body." She looked at them both, her eyes lit up with the most excitement Phadre had ever seen from her. "Like, a dead body? That's pretty neat."

Jiarna's eyes went wide, and one thing was clear on her face. Her recent anger had melted away, and for the moment, there was only excitement and intrigue.

THE EXAMINARIUM WAS A COLD, damp basement filled with sharp chthonic odors, the scent cut only slightly by the acrid smoke of burning lamp oil and the sting of harsh chemicals.

Jiarna loved it.

Inspector Stendall led her and Phadre in, making apologies for bringing a lady into such a gruesome place.

"Nothing of the sort," Jiarna said. "This is a place of valued work. I appreciate that."

"And, again, I apologize for not listening to you

before. But now with two of these bodies, I'd appreciate any insight we can get. Caden!"

A heavy-set bear of a man in a leather apron came over to them. "These are the consultants? Pleasure. Caden Orrickall."

Jiarna offered her hand. "Likewise, doctor."

A small smile appeared through his thick beard. "I don't normally claim that title."

"But it is appropriate, no?"

"I hold three letters of mastery, so, yes," he said. "But whatever this is, it exceeds the knowledge I've gained from those."

"We're happy to help," Phadre said.

"This way." He brought them over to steel tables, each with a draped, withered body on them. "Do these match the body you two found in Invell Valley? I've already sent a letter to the sheriff out there, but it will be at least a week before I hear back."

"Rather," Jiarna said, taking out her eyepiece. She peered at both of the bodies through it, but saw nothing unique about the numinic flow around them.

"What is that?" Orrickall asked.

She handed it over. "It's a lens treated with magic sensitive salts. It allows one to see numinic disruptions."

He looked through it, examining the bodies, and then at Phadre. "Oh, he's a mage. Fascinating. Where did you get this?"

"It's my own design," she said. "I study magic without having any affinity for it myself, so I needed the tools."

"Brilliant," he said. "But not helpful in this case, it seems."

"No," she said.

"So this isn't magic?" Inspector Stendall asked.

Phadre took the answer. "It's not, strictly speaking, magic, no. Not in the sense of what I practice. But what we traditionally call 'magic' is just one facet of a wider range of mysticism, and all we've done is ruled out the most common type."

"Like I told you, specs," Orrickall said. "This is nothing natural."

"But 'not natural' and 'not magic' still leaves a wide range of the unknown," Jiarna said. "Have you performed autopsical examination yet?"

"On the first, yes," he said, pointing to what Jiarna presumed was Missus Grindel's body. Like Mister Dreshin, it was an eyeless, desiccated husk, barely identifiable as the person she once was. "I was just getting to Mister Underman here."

"May I assist?" Jiarna asked.

"Happily," he said. "I have aprons and gloves in that wardrobe there."

"Underman?" Phadre asked as Jiarna dressed for examination. "I don't remember there being an Underman on the caravan."

"No, he's a local fellow," Inspector Stendall said. "Shopkeeper who lives in the Stonepost District. Spoke to his closest family— a pair of cousins— said he hasn't left the city in over a year."

"And any personal connection with Missus Grindel?" Jiarna asked.

"Not that we've determined yet," Stendall said. "She lived in Levin. Might have had cause to go to his shop, it was in the business district on the south side. Beyond that, it's hard to say."

Jiarna furrowed her brow. "And do we have any report about either of them, how they seemed shortly before their deaths?"

"What do you mean?" Stendall asked.

"Their health, their behavior," Jiarna said. "Was there anything abnormal we should know?"

"We can't rule out some form of pathogen," Orrickall said as he took a charcoal stylus from behind his left ear and jotted a note in his journal.

"Could we be carriers?" Phadre asked.

"You're thinking this is some sort of plague?" Stendall asked.

"Not necessarily," Jiarna said. "But I think it would be irresponsible not to consider it. And, yes, dear, if it were, we have certainly risked exposure. I would argue, though, that Mister Dreshin showed no signs of illness a mere hour before we found his body."

"True," Phadre said. "And Missus Grindel or Mister Underman?"

"They had both been seen by neighbors or others on the same day. No one reported anything odd. But if this is a sickness—"

"Which it may be," Jiarna said, coming back to the bodies with an apron, gloves and goggles on, her numinic eyepiece in place under the goggles. "But like Doctor Orrickall said, this does not seem like anything natural." She picked up a scalpel. "Ready to begin, doctor?"

THERE WAS, indeed, nothing natural about the state of either body. They were not merely withered, dried husks. It was as if they had been hollowed out. Organs were blackened and shriveled, so dry they almost crumbled to dust at Jiarna's touch.

"It looks like whatever process did this to them originated from the inside," she told Orrickall.

"That was my feeling," he said. "Like the body… consumed itself. Can magic do that?"

"Quite possibly," she said. "Am I right, darling?"

"Well, I imagine so," Phadre said. "I wouldn't know how to do that, exactly, but certainly I think it could be done."

"But you said this wasn't magic," Inspector Stendall said.

She tapped her eyepiece. "There is no sign of an abnormal numinic shift here. If these people had been assaulted by a mage— someone with magical ability like Phadre— it would leave markers I would be seeing right now."

"Like scar tissue?" Orrickall asked.

"An apt comparison, yes," she said. "Like scar tissue on the magical fabric surrounding them."

"So, what can you determine?" Stendall asked. "Besides ruling out magic?"

"Well," she said, moving her attention to the bones. Even those felt like ash. "It's not like any illness I've heard of, but I'm not enough of an expert on disease to truly eliminate that as a possibility. Though my instinct tells me it's not."

"Can you eliminate murder?" Stendall asked.

"Not at all," she said. "In fact, I think the most sensible thing to consider is that this was done with deliberate intent, and presumably malicious. Phadre?"

"Yes, dear?"

"The night in Invell Valley, we most definitely heard a scream, yes?"

"Quite certainly," he said. "That's what drew us to the body."

"Yes," she said. "A scream like someone being attacked." Though she had thought it had been a feminine voice, despite the body being Mister Dreshin.

She could only reconcile that with observer error; she had interpreted what she heard incorrectly. "And we know Dreshin seemed to all observation in fit health before, so this… whatever it is…"

"It's someone doing this to people," Stendall said. "So, murder."

"I'm inclined to think that," she said. "A mystical murder, most likely."

"And we have to presume the murderer was on the caravan with us," Phadre said. "Either passenger or crew."

"Or cargo," Jiarna offered.

"What do you mean?" Phadre asked.

"Not sure," she said, looking closer at the destroyed liver. "Just don't want to needlessly eliminate options."

"A Caldemane Caravan?" Stendall asked, taking out a notebook and stylus. "When did you arrive?"

"Twenty-ninth of Soran," Jiarna said.

"That's a place to start. I'll get a writ for the manifest from Caldemane.

"Doctor Orrickall, can we take some tissue samples with us back to Inchellian House? We have both equipment and additional expertise that could prove useful in isolating what may have caused this."

"Be my guest," Orrickall said, bringing sample jars over. "Can I call on you both there if I have further questions?"

"Of course," Phadre said. "Glad to help."

They finished collecting the samples, and Jiarna cleaned herself up and loaded the jars in a satchel to carry back to the house.

"I could help with that," Phadre said as they walked.

"I know you could, darling, but I fear you could

unwittingly contaminate the numinic fabric of the samples, and that could damage the work."

"Hmm," Phadre said. "What's his name— Laslin— he said I may have been affecting my own observations as well. Perhaps I should be the subject and not the observer."

"Darling," Jiarna said, realizing his mood was darkening. "I hope you know how much value you bring to both our work, as well as my own personal joy. Your ability as a mage is invaluable to the work."

"But we need to be aware—"

"Of all variables and influences! It's basic science, my love."

They reached the house and she made straight for the lab. "You're thinking something specific," Phadre said, following after her.

"I am," she said. "Either as an answer, or a thing to eliminate. Presuming that the group's experiments have proven accurate." She took out the sample jars and lined them up on the table.

"Tell me," he said.

She went over to the workbench where Achariatt and Jovi had been working on their latest project, exactly the device she needed.

"The psychic compass?" Phadre asked.

"A crude test, of course," she said. Ideas were bubbling through her, and she struggled to get them coherently into words "But consider— we have eliminated *numinic* magic, we have considered disease unlikely. What remains? The first thing I can think of is some form of telepathic assault."

"On the whole body?"

"Well, perhaps telepathic is the wrong word," she said, the excitement building. If this worked, as she suspected it might, it would not only give her a direction to focus her investigation into the deaths, but also demonstrate the value of the psychic compass itself. "But that energy— the force of Will, to use the term Geordine prefers— perhaps it has the same source. Perhaps what it is capable of is far beyond what we know. Telepathy is only the surface."

"You said 'perhaps' three times. You are deep into speculation."

"True," she said, bringing the compass over to the table. "Which is why I want to test my theory."

She held the compass— a device Jovi and Achariatt had built with intricately cut crystals and precisely chosen rare metals— close to the jars.

"Well?"

The needle of the compass swung hard toward one jar, and then back the other way to another, and then started vibrating rapidly. Too fast for Jiarna to see.

"I would say this confirms my theory that this involves psychic energy," she said, looking over to Phadre. "I mean, we'll need to develop more precise methodology, determine a scale for reading the energy, perhaps using the same principles—"

"Jiarna!" Phadre shouted.

She looked back at the compass. The needle was now spinning at an alarming rate while sparks crackled and snapped from it. Suddenly, the needle and the crystal housing burst in a flash of light and flame. Jiarna screamed and dropped it.

It shattered on the ground, still smoking as scorched shards of crystal and shrapnel.

Destroyed.

CHAPTER SIX

"THIS IS COMPLETELY UNACCEPTABLE, MISS KAY!"

Jiarna had expected to be chastised by Professor Salarmin, but she was more than a little surprised how brutally public he had made the whole affair. She had made no attempt to hide what she had done— there was no way to do that— and on reporting it he had called the entire house together in the sitting room.

He had been fuming mad, at first shouting for everyone to come down, then pacing back and forth with such ferocity that he was sure to wear holes through the blue and yellow Ghaladi carpet.

"Explain it to me again," he snarled as everyone was there, holding the scorched pieces of the destroyed compass in his hand.

"Well, we—" Phadre started.

"Be quiet, Mister Golmin. I want to hear her explain it."

"As I said, we were contacted by the constabulary regarding their mysterious corpses."

"Do we serve the constabulary of this city, Miss Kay?" He stormed around the room, and pointed to

Kennick. "Is that our function, Mister Mallin? Is this something we do?"

"Not something we've done before, sir," Kennick said.

"No, not something we do. We are here serving the college, serving science, and as needs be, serving the interests of the patrons who support us."

"And what about a threat to the community?" Jiarna asked. She may have damaged the psychic compass, and compromised the work Jovi and Achariatt had done, and for that she was truly sorry, but she refused to apologize for doing the right thing as far as analyzing a potential danger. "If something is happening in the city that is beyond the understanding of almost everyone, save the people in this room, we have a respons—"

"We have a responsibility to the people who fund us," he said.

"I still want to know how she broke it," Achariatt said. "Can you go back through that?"

"Carelessness is how she did it," Professor Salarmin said. "Touching things that were not hers to touch."

"Sir, you should not—" Phadre started to say.

"You should have taken steps to prevent this girl's foolishness!" Salarmin shouted.

"Prevent her what?" Phadre asked, his eyes narrowing.

"Taken the compass away from her and escorted her out of the lab. That's what anyone sensible would do!"

"This girl—" Phadre said through tight teeth. Jiarna didn't need her eyepiece to know that he was swirling with a draw of numina. "Jiarna has a better understanding of every single theory and concept behind this work than—"

"One more word, Mister Golmin, and the both of you will be on the street, drummed out of the college faster than a clap of lightning!"

Jiarna grabbed Phadre's arm, hoping to cool him down, as much as she loved him staunchly defending her. But she did recognize she had damaged someone else's work, and that alone was worthy of chastisement. She had set Jovi's and Achariatt's work back, and that was on her to make right.

"I'll do what's needed to get the compass project back on track," she said.

"You will indeed," Professor Salarmin said. "But I don't want you in the lab for now. Instead, I have a different task for you, one to keep you out of mischief."

"I still—" Achariatt started.

"In my office on campus, I have a crate of journals and diaries of noted practitioners of mystic arts. I've not had the opportunity to properly go through them and catalog their value. That is where your afternoons and evenings will be spent, Miss Kay. And you, Mister Golmin, will engage in whatever grunt work Mister Njien and Chrenistinajovikam require for the immediate duration of their rebuilding of the compass in time for our presentation to the Lord of Yin Mara. Including being responsible for their household chores on top of your existing duties."

"Yes, sir," Phadre said.

"Of course," Jiarna said.

"Perhaps that will keep the two of you occupied enough to not need side projects with the constabulary," he said. He handed the broken pieces to Achariatt. "See what you can make of this, Mister Njien. Ask Golmin and Kay for whatever you need. *Whatever.* I'm going to go meet with the factors for our patrons and see what sort of extension we can muster for our presentation. Mister Mallin, with me." He went out the door, and Kennick scrambled to get boots and a coat to catch up with him.

"That is the fifth most angry I've ever seen him," Geordine said quietly. "I'm going to have to make a new chart, I think." She scurried off upstairs.

Jovi, who had spent the entire dressing down shrinking in the corner, came quietly over to Jiarna and put a hand on her shoulder. "I'm sorry."

"No, I am," Jiarna said. "I did, in fact, damage your work and set you all back. I deserve whatever rebuke you give me."

"I am upset," Achariatt said. "But fascinated as well, because whatever you did, well, it's at least proof of concept. You used it and got a reading, yes?"

"I had a reaction," Jiarna said. "I don't know if I would call that a reading."

"A strong reaction, though. Go over it all again. Every detail."

"Right," Jiarna said, thinking through it all. She had yet had the chance to properly journal and chronicle her observations. "We had the tissue samples from the two dead bodies, borrowed from the examinarian's office. I carried them here myself because I didn't want Phadre's numinic flow to cause any inadvertent corruption of the data. My eyepiece had already showed, though, that whatever had killed the two people had no numinic traces."

Jovi nodded, "So of course you wanted to try the psychic compass, see if it gave off any energy that was consistent with how we think telepathy works."

"Logical, yes," Achariatt said. "And when you brought the compass near the samples?"

"The reaction was intense. The needle moved wildly, and the crystals in the housing sparked."

"That is very interesting indeed," Achariatt said. "That means we are on the right track with the crystal array. Perhaps we've underestimated how many we should use. Or overestimated it."

"Or those particular samples had a stronger energy than we were prepared for," Jovi said. "We need to do further work."

"I'll help however you need," Jiarna said. "The professor was overly crude about it, but I accept the chastisement."

"Where are those samples?" Jovi asked.

"Still in your lab," Phadre said. "We can get rid of them—"

"By no means!" Achariatt said. "I think you were right about one thing: they are very worthy of study. Chren, I think if we use them, we can help establish a stronger baseline of what energy outputs we are going to be expecting."

"What we built is *too* delicate to be useful," she offered.

"Yes, exactly," Achariatt said. His face brightened. "In fact, Jiarna, your carelessness may have saved us embarrassment later."

"Well, that's good," Phadre said, putting a comforting hand on Jiarna's shoulder. She reached up and took his hand. "Failure and reformation of hypothesis is the standard we should always follow."

"Indeed," Achariatt said. "Chren, let's be about it."

She looked hesitantly at Jiarna and Phadre. "I was on kitchen duty this evening, but—"

"We have it," Jiarna said.

"Gladly," Phadre said. "Neither of us so vain to not take our turn to support you two succeeding."

They went off to the lab, leaving Jiarna alone with Phadre.

"I appreciate you defending me," she told him. "But, please, lay into me and tell me how foolish and cocksure I was."

"Nothing doing," he said.

She looked askance at him.

He continued. "Did you have an unintended consequence? Of course. But, again, that's science. You know that. The setback has caused us trouble, and we will take our lumps with dignity. But I will never chastise you for your relentless pursuit of the truth."

She smiled despite her sour mood. "I do adore you, dearly."

"Fortunately, my feelings are reciprocal." He kissed her with a significant amount of ardor and intent, and then moved said kissing to her neck.

"My," she said, pulling away, despite being very interested in following up where those kisses were going.. "I should make dreadful mistakes more often."

He kissed her once more. "Let's follow up on that later. For now, we have meals to prepare. We will always have more mistakes to rectify."

THE PROFESSOR WAS deadly serious about the crate of journals. He delivered them to the house the next morning and told Jiarna he wanted them all— at least fifty— cataloged for their usefulness by the end of the week. "And mind you, they're a mélange of personal journals with possible elements of magical studies and other notes mixed in. So, you'll need to carefully go through them all. No skimming."

That made it clear, he expected her to read through it all.

It would have been better for her if the journals held

absolutely nothing of value. But as she read through them, they were exactly what she feared: several personal recollections of minutiae of daily life from three centuries ago by tiresome old men with at best, a passing interest in the science of mystical arts. But then, within each one, there would be some kernel of insight, some notable observation, that gave the entire thing a new value that she had to note.

For example, Jescor Hidd spent a decade in the tenth century travelling through the wilds of Waisholm and Bardinæ, roughly following the path Brenium had taken a millenium earlier. But Brenium had the foresight to compile his thoughts and observations into something organized and cohesive. Hidd's journals were mostly a rambling free verse of every bodily function he engaged in on his journey. She admired the apparent thoroughness, for no meal, defecation or copulation was left out for the entire ten-year period. But buried between a rumination of the sexual vigor of the Bardinæ, (Jiarna found his attempts to quantify his experience with objective values of measurement a bit disturbing) and his suppositions on how specific local delicacies affected the consistency of bowel movements (Hidd had developed a system of analysis of his remains that had an intellectual rigor that Jiarna respected, even though she was deeply uninterested in reading such details), there was a rather fascinating examination of the runic magic of Bardinæ, and the way it might correlate with symbols associated with ancient power in Old Waish.

Most of the journals were like that, though none quite as obsessed with the scatological as Hidd. On top of that, the journals themselves were often ill-kept, musty-smelling and damaged. The work of going through them made her head pound, probably from exposure to whatever old molds festered in between the pages.

She reminded herself that this was supposed to be a punishment, and while she did not feel she deserved such a thing, she resolved herself to do the work with the same diligence she put into any other work she would undertake. In addition to the cataloging, she bought a fresh journal and transcribed any passage she found meaningful or insightful. Despite the hardship of the work, she did recognize the value behind it. While she read through a significant amount of nonsense, burning lamp oil late into each night and suffering from the lack of sleep, every single journal had something she found notable.

Then there was the one that was half in another language. After asking the rest of the group, she determined that it was not a language anyone else in the house knew, but Achariatt said it looked like Imach. She checked with Professor Salarmin, he identified the writing as using an Imach alphabet, but he wasn't familiar with the specific language.

"I can tell you it isn't Ghaladi or Mahaban. Likely one of the northern kingdoms. If it's got anything of value to us, then it's most likely Mocassan, which is the only Imach nation where mystical studies are taken even remotely seriously."

"Does anyone on campus know Mocassan Imach?" she asked.

"Not that I know of," he said. He put the book back in her hands. "Do what you can."

About two-thirds of the book was in this other language, so she focused on the parts in Trade, which involved the details of travel up the Acserian coast, then to New Acoria in Napoli, and ending with a planned journey to southern Druthal at the end of the journal. Nothing of note there. If there were aspects notable to mystical science, it was buried in the Imach text. Some of those sections included sketches of plants or geometric shapes that seemed promising, but without the accompanying text, it was hard to say.

She flipped through it one more time to make sure she hadn't missed anything.

One of the sketches she had missed on her first pass — the pages had stuck together— jumped out at her.

It was a drawing of a dead body, which looked *exactly* like the ones in the examinarium.

She didn't even know what time it was— deeply late into the night— but she let out a cry of surprise as she took the journal and ran out of the library toward Phadre's room.

She almost ran straight into the tall, hairy fellow in his skivs, and barely managed not to scream in terror.

"Did you find something?" he asked.

"You— you're… you're Laslin?" she asked back.

"Maybe," he said. "I…" He tapped his head. "Some of this got lost."

"I'm sorry," she said. "I can't imagine what that's…"

"What did you find?" he asked, pointing to the book.

"It's—" she felt oddly compelled to show him. "It's an old journal in an Imach language."

He took the book from her and looked through the pages, muttering, *"enacci a lharrum, ihlalrhan assah"*.

"You can read it?" she asked.

"I guess I can," he said. "When did I learn Mocassan Imach?"

She flipped the book to the pages with the image. "What does it say here?"

His eyes went wide. "Oh, that's gruesome! I don't—"

"Sorry," she said. The poor man was fragile, she had been told. He shouldn't have to look at pictures of dead things. She started to take the book away.

"No, no," he said. "Let me see." His eyes narrowed as he flipped through the pages. "Oh, that's… that's terrible."

"What does it say?"

"This is about two hundred years old, right?" He pointed to one set of figures. "That's a date in the Mocassan calendar, and that's 1007 by our reckoning. And it looks like whoever wrote this was in Bahema at the time—"

Bahema was a coastal city in Amida Province in Acseria. That matched the parts she could read, Amida Province was the last place the author was in before heading to the Napolic Islands.

"What happened with the bodies?"

"Several people were found dead, looking like this," Laslin said, his finger shaking. "And the people in the city, they blamed the fellow who wrote this. But he knew it was someone else."

"Someone?" she clarified. "A person did this?"

"He writes, 'I almost caught him before he leaped away, his last victim in my arms.' And then he talks about having to flee from the angry mob who thought he was the killer…"

Laslin put the book back in her hand, his own trembling.

"Are you all right?" she asked.

"No, most certainly not, but… that… that isn't on you. The crystals shattered on you, didn't they? Yes, shattered." He stumbled off down the hall.

She held the book close to her chest, her heart breaking.

She would tell Phadre in the morning. For now, she had been up too late, and needed to rest. But this proved one thing: whatever this was that had killed three people, it had happened before. It would be irresponsible of her to ignore that, if she had knowledge that could help.

Her sense of moral obligation to science demanded no less.

CHAPTER SEVEN

"TWO HUNDRED YEARS AGO, IN AMIDA," Jiarna said, showing the journal to the rest of the group at lunch, save Kennick, who was lecturing. "This happened at least once before."

Phadre looked at the pages, not sure what to make of it. The sketches certainly looked like the bodies they had seen, but the foreign writing was completely beyond his ability to figure. "How do you know what it says?"

"Laslin read it," she said as she laid out bowls of cabbage soup and bread. "He told me—"

"Wait, wait," Chren said. "You talked with Laslin?"

"I ran into him in the hallway— I was working late, and he's clearly adopted a nocturnal habit— and he asked what had me so excited..."

"How was he?" Geordine asked.

"Oh, very clearly shattered," Jiarna said. "Whatever accident he had damaged the element of his mind that helps him understand who he is. He didn't even know he could read Mocassan Imach until he did."

"Is it possible, dear," Phadre said, not sure of the best way to phrase things, but knowing that she would have respect for a direct statement sent. "That Laslin does not read Mocassan Imach, but told you some delusional story?"

"Yes, of course it is," Jiarna said plainly. "I am absolutely taking into account that my data is being filtered and could be corrupted. It would be foolish not to acknowledge that."

"But yet?" Achariatt asked.

"It is still highly likely that a matching series of deaths occurred in the vicinity of the author of this journal. Now, Laslin might have been lying about his translation. Laslin might have translated honestly but inaccurately. Even presuming accurate translation, the author might be unreliable in their account. They even could have been the perpetrator. But this still gives us new information."

"To what end?" Chren asked. "You've already been reprimanded for focusing on this."

"Not to mention damaging our project," Achariatt said.

"You don't think it's worth knowing what is happening?" Jiarna asked.

"My opinion here is surely considered biased," Phadre said. "But I agree with Jiarna. There is a potential danger here, and three people have died. If it is of a mystical nature—"

"If," Geordine said sharply. "We don't know if that is the case."

"We know we don't know what is causing it," Jiarna said. "But we also know that it is beyond the capability of the constabulary to understand it."

"And perhaps us," Geordine said. "Maybe we can't know—"

"No," Jiarna said. "I will not accept that. I accept there are things we do not understand. I accept that there are things that will not be understood in my lifetime. But that there are things that we will never understand? No, ma'am. I will not bow my head in defeat to ignorance."

"Ignorance is the enemy we will always face," Phadre added. "But it will yield to its betters."

Chren looked at the pictures in the journal and shuddered. "All right, let's presume this is worthy of exploration. We don't have time, as we need to finish our psychic compass project."

"Yes," Jiarna said, her eyes lighting up. "You do, and I know you've finished a new prototype."

"That doesn't mean—" Achariatt started.

"Which means you should conduct a proper field test."

Phadre could see it on everyone's faces. She had piqued their interest.

"Go on," Chren said.

"We know that the tissue samples of the victims set off the compass."

"Destroyed it," Geordine said. She picked up the journal and started flipping through it idly.

"Perhaps because it was so close to the source," Jiarna said, raising her voice as she went into the other room. "But what if we tried something more methodical, while also determining if the compass is the valuable detection tool we are hoping it can be."

"Which would be?" Achariatt asked.

Jiarna came back with a rolled-up chart. She unrolled it out on the table— a map of the city. "We take the cart, load in with the compass, and ride through the city, moving through key centers of each district. I've already mapped it out. We take readings as we go, which would allow us to get a sense of the, shall we say, psychic baseline of the city and find the hotspots of energy throughout."

"And if one of those hotspots is the source of these killings?" Chren asked.

"Then that is also useful data," Phadre said. "But even if it isn't, I think you can agree it's a worthwhile process. I will help however I can."

"Do you know how to drive a mulecart?" Achariatt asked.

"As a matter of fact, I do," Phadre said.

"Hidden talents," Jiarna said with a sly smile.

"Good," Achariatt said, even though his face betrayed annoyance. "Because I will have to insist that Chren and I handle the readings as we do this. Jiarna, you'll need to be our scribe."

"Gladly," Jiarna said.

"What's wrong, Chari?" Geordine asked Achariatt, still frowning over the map. "Sounds like everyone wins. You can get data, and Jiarna might find her psychic killer. Very exciting. We might even get killed."

"Because even if there wasn't a psychic killer that we could find with this method, this is actually a very useful project to test the compass," Achariatt said. "And I'm angry with myself, I should have thought of it."

"Our whole purpose here is to think of things for each other," Jiarna said. Together, they were stronger, and together they could figure it out.

JIARNA'S PLAN had begun quite promisingly, and Phadre enjoyed the process of being out in the air on the mulecart. He had not spent much of his time at Inchellian House acquainting himself with Fessie, the mule— care for her had been largely been Geordine's province— but she was a sweet and well-tempered animal who was easy to interact with. Geordine had come along on this project, he thought, just to supervise his behavior with Fessie. She obviously had a lot of affection for the animal. In her place, he would be just as apprehensive of a new driver. He endeavored to be worthy of their trust, both Fessie and Geordine.

"I think the problem is we took the directive of 'compass' too literally," Achariatt said after an hour of driving and charting. "Our device gives us directionality but not intensity."

"Presuming intensity is measurable," Chren said.

"Well, it must be," Achariatt offered. "We're already noting, as directionality changes, if the needle swings aggressively or lazily. We've been seeing plenty of both."

"And I've been noting it," Jiarna said.

Geordine looked over Jiarna's shoulder, and then made her own notations in the city map they were using. "This data is fascinating. There are definitely strong locus points of whatever you're tracking throughout the city."

"Indeed," Achariatt said, then he called out the next reading to Jiarna. "I've already made a few hypotheses regarding what we're seeing here."

"Go on," Chren said.

"First, of course, is that our entire premise is incorrect and what we are measuring has nothing to do with psychic energy or telepathy."

"Agreed," Chren said. This had been the fundamental flaw in the work they had been doing on this: all of their theories were based on previous work and writings that could all be bad fruit of a dead branch. They had yet to have positive confirmation with a known telepath, since known telepaths were exceedingly rare. "Beyond that?"

"Two possibilities," Achariatt said. "Either there are several strong telepaths in the city, serving as 'high heat' sources that we're measuring— for lack of a better term."

"A good term. I like it," Chren said.

"Or we have many more people who are weak telepaths, a much higher percentage of the population than we theorized, which creates the illusion of locus points. Without a measurement of intensity, it's hard to be sure."

"But using needle swing intensity as a gauge has shown some sources are stronger," Jiarna offered. "We know that mages have variable levels of raw *numina* channelling abilities. Some can handle much larger *barin* flow than others, and that tends to translate in great power levels. Darling, make a note that in the future we should do a proper study of measuring *barin* flow in a wide sample of mages."

"Noted," Phadre said. "We also don't know the full extent of telepathic power or how that's identified or nurtured."

"Expand on that," Geordine said.

Phadre reined Fessie to a stop on the side of the road— they were going down the Old Troop and Post Road that led near the Silver Apple District, home to wealthier merchants and minor noblilty— to look at everyone.

"Consider that many people might be just telepath enough to never fully realize what they are. We've all known folks who have an innate sense of people. The merchant who knows exactly the sort of thing you want to buy. The new acquaintance who immediately feels like an old friend."

"Possibly," Achariatt said. "They might be using telepathy so softly, so instinctively, they might not realize what they are doing because they don't have any reference that what they experience is different from the norm."

"That doesn't make sense," Chren said.

"Let me put it in terms you can relate to," Phadre said. "My cousin could not distinguish colors. Red, green, blue… all the same to him."

"Fascinating," Chren said.

"Now, imagine that my cousin's experience was the norm. Most people don't see colors, don't talk about them. But you, who sees a full spectrum of color, would have access to a level of information most people do not."

Her brow furrowed in thought. "Yes. But in this theoretical world, no one talks about color, there are no words for it. And the person who does see color would have little reason to suspect that their experience was different from everyone else's."

"Unless their attention is called to it, which maybe only happens to the strongest of telepaths," Achariatt said. "I wish we had something concrete to work with instead of just theory."

"We might," Jiarna said. "Look."

Phadre followed her gaze to the compass, which was vibrating wildly, the needle in intense oscillation.

"That seems rather significant," Chren said.

"Directionality and intensity," Jiarna said, and jumped off the wagon, dashing in exactly the direction the needle was pointing. Her path led directly to a high fence, the back of someone's property, which she scaled over without a moment of hesitation. In the count of two breaths, she was out of sight.

"What just happened?" Geordine asked.

"Did she really just do that?" Chren asked.

"We should follow her," Phadre said, getting off the wagon. "Bring the compass."

"We should what?" Achariatt asked. "Are you both mad?"

"Determined," Phadre said. "Come along, unless you wish for a fence to hold back the march of discovery."

Achariatt picked up the compass and moved toward the fence cautiously. "You're certain we won't get in trouble?"

"Absolutely."

"I KNEW we would get in trouble," Achariatt said. "I knew it."

The five of them sat on a bench in the constabulary stationhouse. Jiarna had not anticipated this turn of events. Geordine was fuming, Jovi trembling. Achariatt's leg was vibrating as he drummed his fingers on the arms of the bench.

Phadre, bless him, was projecting nothing but serenity.

"You two again," Inspector Stendall said as he came onto the work floor, the two patrol officers who had brought them in at his heels. "You've got a cadre now, it seems."

"We're a cadre now?" Geordine snapped. "What the blazes— pardon, sir— what is this you've stuck us with?"

"Inspector," Jiarna said, putting as much honey as she could into her tone. "As you are aware, we all researchers with the university. We were taking readings critical to our research—"

"That weird box they had," one of the officers said.

"We had a reaction that was unprecedented, and in our zeal, we may have forgotten the usual bounds of propriety."

"And property," Stendall said. "You're lucky Missus Hinderlay only had her staff boy run for constables. If Mister Hinderlay had been home, I reckon he would have brought out his crossbow."

"Surely it wouldn't have come to that," Jiarna said.

"Do you know what she said in her report?" Stendall said. He pointed to Jovi and Achariatt. "She said 'foreigners tried to invade my home.'"

Jiarna scoffed. "Patently ridiculous, we never went near her actual home."

"Jiarna!" Geordine said. "Stop being so absurd. We have been arrested."

"Have we?" Jiarna asked. "My study of law is lacking, but while we're here in the stationhouse, we are not in holding. We have not been processed by staff, nor have we been granted a Justice Advocate to plead on our behalf."

"Miss Kay—" Stendall started.

"I understand we gave Missus Hinderlay a fright, and I will personally tender an apology. Phadre and I will do that together."

"Hmm, yes," Phadre said. He was serene, but his thoughts were clearly elsewhere.

Jiarna continued. "But unless your intent is to actually arrest us, I would presume we can go once we have our property returned to us."

"Your property?" Stendall asked.

"She means the wagon, our animal and the psychic compass," Phadre said.

"The what?"

Phadre sighed. "The weird box, as he said."

"It is a weird box," the officer said.

"It's a critical element of our work," Achariatt said quietly. "We… sir… we're supposed to present it to the lords of the city. You can ask our professor."

"I intend to," Inspector Stendall said. He shook his head. "Fine, you are free to go, provided you do issue that apology *in writing* to Missus Hinderlay—"

"Of course," Jiarna said.

"I will check in with her, and Saint Marian help me if she did not receive it, and is not fully satisfied with your contrition."

"I will be exceptionally contrite," Jiarna said.

"I'd like to see that," Geordine muttered bitterly. It was clear that Jiarna would have to work to make amends with her colleagues. Jovi was still terrified, and that would require significant reparation as well.

Stendall scowled at them all. "You can have your property back— at least the wagon and the animal— after you pay an impound fine."

"Which will be?" Phadre asked.

Stendall looked to his clerk, who shrugged. "Seven crowns ten?"

"Seven?" Achariatt asked, his voice going up an octave.

"Seven crowns ten," Stendall said with firm indignation.

Phadre nodded and stood up, taking coins out of his pocket and counting them. Bless him. He had it covered. Jiarna made a note to reimburse him, and thank him personally when they were alone.

"And… the compass?" Acharriat asked.

"If it really is as critical as you say," Stendall said, taking the coins from Phadre, "Then your Professor can explain that when he comes to claim it."

Achariatt and the others trudged out of the stationhouse, all of them going on about how the

Professor was going to react. As they all were clearly upset with her, Jiarna thought it best to stay with Phadre as he went out back to get the wagon and mule. His mood was hard to read, but he had every reason to be upset, even if he was masking that in front of the rest of the group.

"I owe you an apology as well," she said as they waited for the wagon. "I let my enthusiasm cloud good sense. So intent on solving the puzzle—"

"Being intent on solving things is what I love about you," he said. "You never need to apologize for that. And you will note I voiced no strong objection at the time."

"Promise me, Phadre, that when you think I am making a grave error in judgment, you will tell me. Regarding my science or daily life."

"You've yet to give me any doubts about your science," he said. "And I'm largely in tune with you regarding your personal life judgment."

She kissed him, quite pleased with that answer.

Mister Orrickall pulled up their wagon.

"Thank you, sir," Jiarna said as Orrickall dismounted, though she was surprised that the examinarium was given such a task. Were the constables in this city so short-staffed that he needed to also perform menial tasks?

"Of course," he said. "But I was hoping for a word. You might have found something?"

"Might is strong," Phadre said. "We've been experimenting with the psychic compass, and rode about the city to get readings. Establish a baseline, you know."

"There was a very strong reaction in the Silver Apple District where we were arrested," Jiarna said. "I can't say it is connected to these murders…"

"Underman's shop has many regular clients from that district," Orrickall said, scratching his chin. "Whatever this is, it has my feathers up, let me tell you. I don't think Stendall is taking it seriously enough."

"Can we help in any way?" Phadre asked.

"I'll look into the Silver Apple District myself," Orrickall said. He took his charcoal stylus out from behind his left ear started writing in his notebook. "What street or household were those readings at?"

"We were apprehended on the grounds of the Hinderlay home?" Jiarna offered. She needed to draft that apology letter as soon as they got back home.

"I think that's Stanway Wood. I'll look around. Something informal that won't hack the Inspector too much."

"Appreciated," Phadre said, taking the man's hand. "We'll help however we can."

"Presuming..." Jiarna said as they got into the wagon, "...that the Professor doesn't us lock us away for this misadventure."

CHAPTER EIGHT

"I CANNOT BELIEVE YOU GOT ARRESTED," Professor Salarmin shouted when he returned from the stationhouse. Kennick stood behind him, carrying the compass, an infuriatingly smug look on his face.

"We were not," Jiarna said, forcing herself to maintain her composure, despite the red-faced fuming from the professor. "We were detained, but not arrested."

"A distinction without a difference," Salarmin said. "Do you know what might have happened if charges were pressed, Miss Kay? Do you have any idea?"

"But they weren't," Jiarna said. "The fact we were even detained instead of allowing us to explain from the beginning is absurd."

"The university would be forced to audit this program, is what would have happened. And that might be fine for you two in the end, but Chren and Achariatt— and myself— are not Druth citizens. Do you have *any* idea what might happen to us if our program in this house was shut down? Maybe my academic reputation might survive, but theirs? And where would they go?"

That shook Jiarna a bit, looking to Jovi and Achariatt. "I'm sorry. I didn't realize."

"Of course you didn't. And all for what, exactly?"

"Actually, the data collected is quite interesting," Jovi said. "I haven't been able to look through it all, but we definitely demonstrated the working value of the compass, identified potential flaws, and have the information to create a rough map of the psychic locus points in the city."

"And frankly, Jiarna has been instrumental in getting us this far," Achariatt added.

Salarmin cooled slightly. "So we have something functional?"

Phadre pursed his lips. "Functional in what sense? We're scratching the surface of the science here, but we aren't even close to charting measurable energy, let alone determining what that might mean."

Geordine scowled. "Why are the purseholders so keen on this one? Is there some sort of function they already have in mind?"

"One that we've been working toward unknowingly?" Phadre added.

Salarmin sighed, and nodded. "Come, sit, sit," he said, leading them to the main table. "What I am telling you is in the strictest confidence."

Jiarna immediately took a seat. This was too intriguing, she had to know more. "Go on."

The rest of the group sat down.

"Some months ago, there was an incident with one of the Sauriyan lords, and while Druth Intelligence and other authorities have kept it quiet, some members of the peerage are aware of what occurred. Including Lord Sweet."

"Which is?" Geordine asked.

"He had apparently fallen under the thrall of a

telepathic villain. A fortunate stroke of luck ended that situation, but for weeks the whole household was held captive by this scoundrel, forced to engage in depravity for his sick pleasure."

Phadre shuddered at that. "Blessed saints protected them."

"As a result, the peerage has been collectively terrified of the idea of something like that happening to them. That they have telepathic infiltrators in their midst."

Phadre gave Jiarna a strong look at that.

"So they want a detection system?" Jiarna asked.

"Detection and protection," Kennick said. "They are desperate for it, and willing to fund our work— significantly—to provide that."

"We've been using the term 'psychic compass' because it sounds a bit more... neutral, and that makes the provosts of the college, who I do need to answer to, a bit less nervous. But it is supposed to be an identifier."

"A bloodhound," Phadre said.

"If you like," Professor Salarmin said.

"All the more reason our data collection was successful and useful," Jiarna said. "We detected a significant psychic presence in the Silver Apple District. If we, with a little more care, return—"

"No," Salarmin said firmly. "You have caused enough chaos with that. No more field tests. Certainly, no more engaging with the constabulary on any project of any sort. This is your focus, friends. Stay in the house, keep working, get it done. Our presentation to the Lords of Yin Mara is in just a few days."

"Yes, sir," Achariatt said before anyone else could speak. "That will be our focus over the next few days. Teach classes, work here, that's it."

"Good," Salarmin said. "Then be about it. It's been a long day. Get some rest, stay focused, then get to work."

"Yes, sir," Kennick said. "I'll see you out."

"Leech," Jiarna muttered as the two of them left.

"You could learn a thing or three from Kennick," Geordine said. "I've got work to do." She stalked off.

"We… do have quite a bit of data to go over," Jovi said, getting up and tapping Achariatt. "We should get to it." Achariatt nodded and left, leaving Jiarna alone at the table with Phadre, who was in a taciturn, contemplative mode.

"Are you upset?" she asked him.

"Quite," he said. "I think we've been more than a little foolish."

"Impulsive," she said. "I don't accept foolish."

"Nonetheless," he said. "We need to proceed with caution in terms of consequences. Both for ourselves, and the other members of this household. Just out of courtesy."

"Are you upset with me?"

"A little," he said. "But it will pass. More, I am troubled by what the professor told us."

"About the psychic attack on the lord? It's…"

"Harrowing, is what it is. What are we, if not our minds?" He stood and approached her. "Look at what happened to Laslin. The idea that… anyone could do that… to our minds? I'm not scared of much, but— that is terrifying."

"I agree," she said. "Which is… perhaps that's why I've been like such a dog on the scent with these bodies. These deaths."

"It's a psychic killer," he said. "We don't know anything else about this thing that's left several bodies except that it kills. And how do we protect ourselves against that? How do we protect our minds, the most precious aspect of ourselves?"

"You said we should strive to understand."

"And we need to," he said. "But we shouldn't do so to our peril."

"And so?" she asked.

"We do like we're told. Focus on the work. Learn how to protect ourselves. Learn everything we can, so we're prepared for whatever might come."

PHADRE DIDN'T SEE much of Jiarna for the next two days, which he briefly worried was due to fault on his part, but he dismissed those fears with the understanding that she, like the rest of the house, was reacting quite normally to the stresses of the presentation on top of their normal duties. In the moments he saw her, he recognized the look in her eye: she was fully immersed in the work. When she was solving a problem, working the science, she shut down in almost all other ways.

He didn't know what he could do to help with the science itself, in these circumstances— this was fully out of his field— so he did what he was able to do, for Jiarna and the rest of the team. He took over all household duties: going to the grocer and other stores for supplies, preparing meals for everyone, cleaning the rest of the house. Part of that he achieved by, in his own mind, cheating. Using magic for household tasks was decidedly unfair, in the sense that no one else could do it that way, and therefore he was creating a new standard that no one else could hope to live up to.

On the other hand, he had managed to get the floors

and tables absolutely gleaming. There was a good deal of satisfaction in that.

If nothing else, should his academic career falter, he could make quite a cozy living offering magical cleaning services. There surely were nobles and other wealthy folk who would pay for such a thing.

Not that he wanted to do that, but there was comfort in knowing the options were there.

"Is there any cheese?"

Laslin stood in the doorway of the kitchen, shredded robe loosely draping his frail body, looking at the sparkling floor like he was afraid to step on it.

"Yes, of course!" Phadre said. "It's good to see you again."

"Right, right," Laslin said. "You have only seen me a couple times. Not the other way around. Cheese?"

"I got a few," Phadre said, opening the ice box. "There's a delightfully sharp sheep cheese from western Patyma. And a Linjari blue-dappled cheese. Do you like those?"

"The blue is mold," Laslin said, gingerly stepping into the kitchen. "But it is tasty."

"Isn't it?" Phadre asked. "Are you interested in some smoked meats? I got the Jaconvale mustard, too."

"That's very thoughtful," Laslin said.

"I was hoping for a word," Phadre said, putting out a plate in front of Laslin. "If that isn't too much trouble."

"Any particular word?" Laslin asked.

"Are you willing to talk to me about the work you were doing? That led to the..." Phadre wasn't sure what delicate word was the best choice here. He opted for bluntness. "Accident?"

"I can't talk about it," Laslin said. He looked down at the plate and scarfed down more cheese.

After a moment, he looked back up. "I'm not trying to be, you know, difficult or evasive. I... *can't* talk about it." He tapped at his head. "It's not really there."

"I'm sorry."

"Yeah," Laslin said. He sliced a piece from another block of cheese— a smooth, bitter cow-milk cheese from eastern Monim— and then held up the slice. "You know, when they make this, gas bubbles form inside the cheese, making these holes. Something... something like that happened in my head, you know. Parts of who I am became... holes."

"I've read the notes you left me," Phadre said. "The parts of you that are left are still brilliant."

"I know," Laslin said, picking up the plate. "I just don't always remember where those are. Like my— I gave it— is there mustard?"

"The Jaconvale," Phadre said, pointing out the jar on the table.

"Oh, that's my favorite," Laslin said, spooning some on his plate. "Little things like that. Like how cheese is made... those stayed. But so much... it's just... gas bubbles."

"I'm sorry," Phadre said.

"I did have things written down, of course." He snapped his fingers as if something had just come to him. "I gave one journal to your lover yesterday."

"My—" Phadre stumbled at that. "Thank you, I'm sure she will find it helpful."

The following morning, the day of the presentation, Phadre woke to several banging noises in the observatory above his room. He quickly dressed and went up there, to find Jiarna in the midst of making bizarre adjustments to the lensescope, the numinic camera, and a few other devices she had assembled together into one singular device, which he couldn't even begin to fully understand.

"I didn't hear you come up here," he said. "Did you take the catwalk across or something?"

"That rickety thing? I wouldn't dare. But I did make a point of being quiet until I reached this point in my assembly that required brute force."

"What are you doing?"

"Having a problem of scale," she said as she bolted two pieces together. She looked up at him. "Is there tea, love? I really could use one."

"I've not gone to the kitchen yet," he said. "I'll get some going shortly, but what are you doing, exactly?"

"Thinking about the next steps," Jiarna said.

"For the assignment the professor put on us?"

"In part," Jiarna said. She stepped away from her work. "All right. So, we develop the compass, in theory, to identify psionic threats."

"Right."

"And then what?"

"Then they're identified," Phadre said.

"And what good does that do anyone if you cannot also neutralize that threat?"

Phadre wasn't sure how to answer that. "Is that what this is?"

"It's an attempt to craft the… *idea* of psionic shielding," she said, holding up a journal. "You know, that's not unlike what Laslin was working on. The initial idea was to present the nobility with not just the means of detection, but the ability to protect someone from psychic influence or attack."

"And Laslin shattered his brain in the process," Phadre said.

"Precisely why I'm not volunteering to self-test," she said. "And like I said, it's a question of scale. I believe I can make something that might make, say, a single room safe from a telepathic attack, but I can't see how to make it bigger to, say, protect an entire household, nor small enough to be practical for individual use. This work right here is more concept than anything. I would need more materials, the cost of manufacture will be ridiculously high. I've already cannibalized several other projects for substitutions."

"That's very interesting, but why the urgency on this?" Phadre asked. "You've clearly been working through the night on this, but it's not part of the presentation, which is today. So why—"

"Why is because we need to have a plan." Jiarna went over to the desk and grabbed the newssheet there. "Because there is a psionic killer in this city and we were definitely tracking it."

Phadre read through, seeing the article of yet another desiccated body being discovered, with the constables having little idea how the death happened, and some assurances that it was not disease and people should not panic.

But what was most of note was where the body was found.

"The Silver Apple District!"

CHAPTER NINE

PHADRE KNEW TIME WAS CRITICAL. THE presentation was in a matter of hours, and Jiarna clearly had energies focused in directions other than being ready for that.

"You did say to tell you if I question your judgment," he said as she walked at her fastest speed toward the constabulary stationhouse. "And I would point out that in a matter of hours we need to be dressed and primped in our very best clothes, including bathed and perfumed and facepainted to be acceptably fashioned for presenting to the city nobility. I have a sense of how long that takes me, and if I extrapolate to the time you'll need, I'm not seeing how we'll be able to be properly ready at half past eleven bells when we're expected to be gathered in the sitting room with the rest of the group to head over."

"It will be challenging," she said, pushing her pace a little faster. It was, frankly, challenging keeping up with her. "Which is why we cannot tarry. We must hurry to the stationhouse, explain the idea to Inspector Stendall and hope he does not dither in his support in that idea—"

"That's a flaw in your logic."

"That is the challenge. All the more reason to bring Mister Orrickall into the conversation, since he is already with us. Maximize our impact in the argument."

"Which is?" She had insisted they charge off with such alacrity, he still wasn't clear to what end.

"To get them to come to the presentation so we can catch the psychic killer—"

"We're expecting them to be there?"

"Yes, of course, it's quite obvious now. Please stop interrupting."

"Certainly."

"Once we get them on board, we rush back to the house, bathe together with some brief but vigorous lovemaking—"

"We'll have time for that?"

"Interruption," she said. "And making the time for that is a priority. We both need a clear head and high spirits for the rest of the day, and I find that is highly effective for achieving both."

"No argument from me."

"I thought not," she said. "And I have my finery already laid out on my bed, I've long devised a system to dress myself with high efficiency, my facepainting and hairwork is minimal in fuss while having maximum— but understated— impact. I am certain that I will be fully prepared to go in time to help you lace your boots."

"I don't need help—"

"You do, love," she said. "And that's a flaw in design, not you. They cannot be done alone."

He decided not to comment on that as they entered the stationhouse. Jiarna charged in, pointing to the clerk with authority. "Is the Inspector in his office? And Mister Orrickall? Where is he?"

"They're both in there," the clerk said, pointing to a back room.

Jiarna went right back there, so Phadre took the moment to say, "Thank you for your help," before following along.

"Good," Jiarna said to Inspector Stendall and Mister Orrickall, who were just drinking tea and eating pastries in what was clearly a room for the constables to relax in. "This saves time. I saw there was a fourth body, clearly there is a serious mystical murderer in this city, and I have a theory of who they are and how we can catch them."

"You… you do?" Orrickall asked. "Based on what?"

"And how do you propose we catch them?" Stendall asked.

"Part of the trap is already laid, I just need you on hand when the moment comes," Jiarna said. She had clearly thought this through far more than she had disclosed to Phadre.

"On hand?" Orrickall asked. "You want both of us?"

"The inspector will be on hand for enforcement of law. And if you can bring officers…"

"Bring them where?" Stendall asked.

"But I would like to have you on hand, Doctor, for your expertise, should it come to that."

"Oh, my expertise," he said, taking the stylus from behind his right ear. He picked up his journal and thumbed through it. "Well, I can't argue with that."

"To where?" Stendall insisted.

"To Lord Sweet's home, where much of the cream of Yin Mara society will be for our presentation. Including the ones I suspect are responsible for these murders."

Phadre could not contain himself. "Who are, exactly?"

"Why, darling, isn't it obvious?" she asked with a raised eyebrow. "It's the Cantons."

PHADRE WAS STILL REELING from the implications of Jiarna's accusation as the group rode out to Lord Sweet's estate, on the outskirts of the city beyond the Silver Apple District. This was not on the mulecart, but a pair of carriages that Lord Sweet had sent for them. Professor Salarmin rode in the first carriage with Kennick, Acharriat and the compass, while Phadre was in the second with Geordine, Chren and Jiarna. Jiarna was stunning in her blue skirt suit with matching cap, capelet and cravat. Such an outfit should have come off as underdressed for a noble audience, but Jiarna made it look regal, fashionable and suitably academic. Plus, impeccably pressed and painted. It was fitting that she was now an absolute model of serenity.

Brief but vigorous had apparently been as effective for her as it had for him.

Phadre had opted for academic robes, with both University of Maradaine and Trenn College regalia on the breast. Geordine's look was similar, though her regalia was from Coanware University, and her usual mad tussle of hair had been combed and properly braided. Chren wore a flowing wrap dress of what Phadre had presumed were iridescent silks from Turjin — or perhaps a facsimile of a traditional Turjin outfit. Not that he had the eye to tell the difference. Before they had gotten in the first carriage, Phadre had noticed that Salarmin and Achariatt had both worn outfits of apparent foreign origin.

"It impresses the nobles," Chren said, as if she had sensed where his thoughts were. "It makes them feel like we are engaged in something truly worldly."

"Well, aren't we?" he asked.

"I suppose," she said. "But it's not like I dress in an *aijhesa* every day."

They reached Lord Sweet's estate, which was isolated from the main road— the highway out past the quarry and beyond the city— by a wooded grove. They rode through a quarter mile of trees before the clearing opened up, and to the household, nestled between two lakes. Several carriages and scores of people were already on the lawn, where tents had been put up, creating a festive atmosphere. The aristocracy of Yin Mara had come out in droves, it had seemed.

"Well now," Jiarna said as they were let out of the carriage. "This is quite exciting."

"How is this plan going to work, now?"

"Very simple," she said. "We know the psychic compass reacts to the remnants of the victims of our killer. We know that it was triggered near the Silver Apple district, and we know that this is the social event for the moneyed people of Yin Mara, and therefore our suspects will be here. Ah, I see them."

Indeed, chatting at a table in the distance with other peers were Lettie and Aister Canton, looking much like they had on the caravan. "They are your main suspects because..."

"Well, they had opportunity. They were on the caravan with us, and then they've been here since. I recall some tension between Missus Canton and Miss Grindel—"

"I saw nothing of the sort."

"Tension between women is subtle, dear," Jiarna said. "Trust that I have an eye for it."

"As you say," he said. "And?"

"And they live in the Silver Apple district. The theory is sound. And now we test it."

"How do we—"

"We're about to demonstrate the psychic compass," she said. "So the demonstration is the field test."

"So we—" was all Phadre managed to say before Professor Salarmin stepped up on a platform stage in the center of the tent pavilion.

"Thank you, thank you, great friends of the sciences and the arts. We are so grateful to be here today to show to you the wondrous and amazing things we have been doing at the Inchellian House. We have several new projects, sure to delight and astonish, but first! I would like you to be dazzled and amazed by our latest edition to our team. Fresh from the University of Maradaine, the magical talents of Mister Phadre Golmin!"

That was not something Phadre had been expecting. He came up to the stage— people were applauding for him, after all, it would be impolite not to— moving close enough to the professor to whisper.

"This part is?" he asked.

"A little showmanship, Mister Golmin. Give them their money's worth."

Their money's worth. Phadre wasn't sure how to do that, exactly. He was an academic, not a circus act.

Circus act.

What would Veranix do here?

"Ladies and gentlemen, and wondrous people of all persuasions," he said with a booming voice. "I've been studying magic intensely all my adult life, so sometimes, I admit, I forget exactly how astounding it can be when seen in person." With that, he conjured up a series of dancing sparks and flames that he swirled into a cyclone. This wasn't the sort of magic he made a habit of doing— it was absurdly crass and showy, and he was going to need to eat half the things on the buffet table after this— but he had learned these as basics in second and third-year practicals. They didn't have a lot of artistry to them, but visually impressive enough for a layperson.

The smattering of applause and squeals of delight proved that point.

"I have been blessed to join my esteemed colleagues and fabulous professor in our endeavors of science, mysticism and understanding, and we have been hard at work developing ways to improve life for you, for the city, and the whole nation, with advancement in all these fields." With each of those, he danced up a flame of a different color, and then pulled them together into a rainbow of fire.

He glanced back, noticing that Jiarna was making small hand signals to the Cantons, and behind them, Inspector Stendall and Mister Orrickall were positioning themselves. He hoped this wasn't about to lead to disaster.

"In a moment, my colleagues will bring forth…"

"Look at that!" Chren shouted, standing next to the psychic compass. Phadre looked over to them again, and caught Jiarna's eye.

She had been looking at the compass, and her gaze traced a line from them to the Cantons.

Her head snapped up. "Got you!"

JIARNA POINTED her finger at the Cantons, the two of them looking like the fools that they were. She had got them, trapped like rats, and the psychic compass had them dead to rights. Pointing directly at them. "We have identified the killers!" she called out.

The crowd exploded in confusion.

"What the—" she heard Professor Salarmin say over the shouts and cries.

"Good people," Phadre said, his voice booming over the crowd. That was a clever trick of magic. "You had hoped we could root out psychic threats, and our compass has done just that! In our midst!"

Inspector Stendall came in and grabbed Aister Canton, but Lettie shrieked and was on her feet when Mister Orrickall moved from behind her. Lettie grabbed her tea and threw it in his face. He cried out and stepped back, and in that opening, Lettie ran.

The woman actually ran away.

Jiarna wasn't going to let that happen.

She charged after the woman, as Lettie pushed her way through the crowd, knocking over a server. Lettie appeared desperate, even crazed, to get away from the party and the constables, not to mention Jiarna.

Saints of knowledge and science, they had done it. They had found the ones responsible for those horrid, mysterious deaths. And when they were caught, Jiarna would know how and why. One more solution for science. One more victory for understanding. One more bit of darkness dragged into the light.

"Get away from me you crazy slan!" Lettie shrieked. "What is wrong with you?"

"This is not the venue to explain that," Jiarna said, grateful she had devoted just enough time to athleticism for the sake of maximizing her body's ability to persevere through work and stress. Though as her chest burned, heart quickened, she made a note to research how to improve lung efficiency for moments of exertion.

If the research did not exist, then she would develop it herself.

Lettie was running down a set of stairs, past the valets and carriages. Clearly, she had no specific plan to escape beyond running. Jiarna, perhaps feeling too much exuberance and zeal in the moment, leaped down the steps to better close the distance.

Mid-air, she realized this was an error.

The heeled boots she had been wearing were not ideal for running, and even less for jumping. She had felt the heel loosen when she jumped, and it was too late to take any action to correct her trajectory.

She landed off-balance, the boot gave out completely, and she tumbled to the ground with a sharp crack from her ankle.

CHAPTER TEN

"JIARNA!" PHADRE SHOUTED AS HE SCRAMBLED past the agitated crowd. Professor Salarmin was shouting to everyone to just be calm.

Before Phadre got any further, a shrill whistle came from Inspector Stendall, bringing a sudden, eerie quiet to the whole affair.

A man in an expensive suit with a silk cravat—whose bearing of authority and ownership made Phadre presume was Lord Sweet, strode over to the platform. "Would someone care to explain what is happening? Why is there this chaos at my home? And the constabulary? I did not request their presence."

"My lord," Professor Salarmin said, stepping up to the man. "Our deepest apologies. There seems to be something of a misunderstanding with the... well, it seems our demonstration of the psychic compass is a bit more—"

"On point?" Kennick offered. Phadre's attention was split five different ways, with most of his emotion focused on Jiarna, who was out of his sight, with too many people between him and her to be able to traverse the distance. He heard her cry out. He was of half a mind to magically shove the people away and force his way through.

Salarmin snapped his fingers at Kennick. "On point, yes, thank you, perfect. You see, my lord, as we discussed, the purpose of the psychic compass is to identify psionic threats, and we seem to have one here in this very event."

"Great saints above!" Lord Sweet said. "Well, that is… troubling. Is that the malefactor, Inspector?"

Inspector Stendall brought Mister Canton over to them, and across the lawn through the throng of people, two of the lord's footmen dragged Missus Canton, while another two helped Jiarna, who seemed to be incapable of using one of her feet.

Phadre threw propriety away and rushed over to her, shoving anyone in his way until he reached her. He grabbed her away from the footman and, despite himself, kissed her. "Are you alright?" he asked when he pulled away.

"Physically, no," she said. "I have caused serious damage to my right ankle. But emotionally… elated." She glanced over to Missus Canton, whose disheveled appearance, complete with grass stains on her skirt and blouse, made it clear she had taken her own tumble, possibly forcibly so at the hands of the footmen.

"But you should be taken to hospital," he told her.

"In due time. I saw one cart already took Mister Orrickall off. I hope he wasn't too injured." Despite saying that, a broad smile crossed her face. "We did it."

"So it would seem," Phadre said, leading her back over to the group at the center. Chren, Geordine and Achariatt were putting the compass in place.

"And that's what led for me to be here, your grace," Inspector Stendall said. "So now let's see what this fuss is all about."

"Well, after all the ado, I am certainly intrigued," Lord Sweet said. "Though I am also quite concerned, as are we all. If there is a psychic threat—"

"My lord, this is absurd!" Mister Canton said. "I am just a successful merchant, a citizen of this city. I'm not some, what do you call it, psychic threat."

"A thing we will determine, sir," Lord Sweet said, holding up two fingers as if to ward off any telepathic attack that might come. "And when we determine it, what preventative measures can we take?"

"We are still working on that part, my lord," Professor Salarmin said quietly.

"Research suggests something as simple as an iron helmet might be helpful," Kennick said.

Everyone scowled at him. There was little data to suggest that actually was helpful.

"It is on our agenda. You recall we lost one of— we have it as a key concern."

"That poor fellow," Lord Sweet said. "Well, we have our apparent malefactors—"

"My lord, I do protest!" Missus Canton shouted.

"Come off it," Jiarna said.

"This woman is in both her moons!" Missus Canton said. "Do not listen to her madness."

"Please," Jiarna said. "Jovi, Achariatt, show them where the psychic compass is pointing."

Chren looked about, a bit out of sorts. "It's not really pointing anywhere."

"What?"

Phadre looked for himself, as did the rest of the people gathered around it, perched on a wooden tripod. Indeed, the needle was just lazily drifting about.

"No, that's not possible," Jiarna said. She reached out as if she intended to turn it with her own hand. "As soon as we opened the case, it was vibrating, giving a very strong reading right at the Cantons. It has to be one of them."

"It isn't now," Acharriat said lamely. "And... I didn't really get a look at it before the commotion started."

Professor Salarmin raised an eyebrow. "Geordine? Chren?"

"I saw it was more active than this," Geordine said. "But I can't speak to it pointing at anyone specifically."

Chren cast her eyes to the ground. "I was watching Phadre perform."

"As was I," Kennick said, unhelpfully.

"Phadre," Jiarna pleaded. "Surely you—"

"I was far away," he said. "I couldn't affirm anything."

"But..." Jiarna said, turning to Missus Canton. "You attacked the constable who was trying to arrest you! You ran!"

"Because you shouted at me like a madwoman!" Missus Canton said, pulling herself away from the footmen holding her. "And I had no idea that he was a constable. He was some random man trying to grab me!"

"But—"

"It's true, Mister Orrickall is our Examinarian, and he was not readily identifiable as a member of our people on sight." Inspector Stendall said, letting go of Mister Canton. "If there is no other evidence—"

"They were on the caravan with us where Mister Dreshin died, and they knew Missus Grindel, the second body, from that ride, and they live in the Silver Apple district near where the fourth body was found."

"Fourth body?" Lord Sweet asked. "You're accusing them of murder."

"Psychically powered murder, my lord," Jiarna said.

"Where they leave the body a dry husk when it is done."

"Oh dear."

"We didn't murder anyone!" Mister Canton said firmly. "When were these other bodies found? Missus Grindel and the others? When were they killed?"

All looked to Inspector Stendall.

"The 17th of Oscan for Missus Grindell, the third on the 4th of Poriman, and then fourth on the 23rd. Yesterday."

"My lord," Mister Canton pleaded. "We spent two weeks after Terrentin at your lake house on the Skane with your nephew and several other guests. Many people here can verify. We weren't even in the city on the 4th!"

"That's true!" an onlooker shouted.

"I saw them!"

"So, we couldn't be your killers!" Missus Canton screamed. "No matter what this maniac or her useless piece of junk says!" With that, she knocked the compass over, its pieces cracking on the ground. Chren shrieked, and Geordine moved to comfort her.

"That does seem to settle it," Lord Sweet said. "It's put a dour cast on the event. Let them go and let's try to have some fun, shall we?" He clapped a few times and musicians started playing. He leaned over to the professor. "Gather yourselves together and let's get something on for dinner, hmm? Something a tad less… accusatory?"

"Of course, my lord." He turned to the team, as Acharriat and Kennick were picking pieces of the compass off the ground. "Well, we need a plan of action. Is it repairable?"

"I think so," Acharriat said. "There are some shattered pieces, but they are replaceable, and—"

"Good. Make a list of what you need, and then you and Chren will get right to work here. Kennick, you take that list and Mister Golmin and head back to the house at best speed. Gather what they need and see what else you can put together to show off to this crowd. Something simple."

"I have something for that, sir," Kennick said proudly.

"Professor, Jiarna is quite injured, I should—"

"You will go with Kennick as I said, Phadre," Professor Salarmin said. "Geordine and I will take her to the hospital, thank you. I have several things to say to you, Miss Kay, and I want Geordi around to remind myself to not say things that are not for ladies' ears."

"Plus, I actually know medicine," Geordine said flatly.

"Yes, that. You all have your instructions, let's be about it."

"I'm sorry," Phadre whispered to Jiarna as he gave her a quick kiss before passing her over to Geordine.

"It... it's fine. I missed something. I had a hypothesis and tested it, and it wasn't right," she said. "But the needle did move."

He told her the only thing he could say. "I believe you. We'll figure it out."

"As you say," she said, squeezing his hands. "We will unravel this mystery."

"Not today, Miss Kay," Professor Salarmin said, brusquely sweeping her up in his arms and carrying her off.

"Come on," Kennick said, knocking Phadre on the shoulder. "This list is gonna send us all around the house. Let's not waste time."

THE RIDE to the hospital was excruciating, in multiple ways. First, and most pressing, was Jiarna's ankle, which throbbed with agonizing pain with every beat of her heart. With Geordine's reluctant help, she had managed to get her boot off without needing to cut it, which would have been an absolute crime. That had alleviated some of the pain, but showed her just how badly she had damaged it. Her entire foot was swollen and engorged, and the skin was a vicious shade of purple.

"That is pretty terrible," Geordine said, and sat in the carriage in a way that she could hold up Jiarna's leg as high as she could bear. It had left her in an indelicate and exposed position with regard to the professor, but she had little concern for the demands of modesty at the moment. Keeping it elevated— Geordine's idea, very well done— had also helped reduce the swelling.

"It might be broken," Geordine said. "Move your toes for me."

"It is deeply painful."

"Perhaps, but a useful diagnosis. Move your toes."

Jiarna respected the lack of sentiment Geordine was showing right now, behaving dispassionately in the interest of proper diagnosis, and did her best to curl her toes, despite the pain.

"Decent," Geordine said. "I can tell you what the doctors will likely do, provided they don't decide amputation is easier."

"Not my preference."

"It's unwarranted, but so many choices they make tend to be. Splint and wrap it, and tell you to stay off of it for at least a week, and then reassess to see if infection or necrosis have set in."

"Lovely," Jiarna said.

"What they won't tell you is to also apply ice to it.

Chilling will reduce the swelling." She sighed and looked to the professor. "Phadre would have been useful here. He could have magically—"

"He's not here, and I would prefer if he and Miss Kay are less directly engaged with each other for the immediate future," Professor Salarmin said.

"That's hardly—" Jiarna started.

"Once again, you have embarrassed us," he said. "Once again, over this absurd business of trying to, what, solve crime? What is it, exactly, you think you are doing, Miss Kay?"

"Sir," she said sharply. "My hypothesis may have been off— perhaps it was not the Cantons, or perhaps they are able to mask their psychic energy in a way that the compass—"

"Still, you insist," he said. He shook his head. "I don't understand—"

"Neither do I, sir. I don't understand how these killings have occurred. I don't understand how it can work, what can be done to stop it, or who is behind it. All I have are disparate scraps of data, and with that I am trying to find a solution."

"That is not your job, Miss Kay. You are here to learn, to teach, to research on the behalf of the entire group, as well as the college. Not solve murders!"

"Who else could solve murders like this?"

"You're not even talking sense," he said. "Frankly, I would be inclined to dismiss you from the program and the house completely."

"She's likely in a lot of pain, sir," Geordine said. "It would make her quite incoherent right now."

"I am not—"

Geordine shot her a look, a warning.

"Not in my right thoughts right now," Jiarna finished. "I apologize, professor, for the incorrect presumption as well as the scene caused by it. Clearly my conclusions were faulty. I must work on that."

She understood that the professor needed some form of apology, and that was one she could stomach without resorting to dishonesty. She had made an incorrect presumption, and her conclusions were faulty. There was no denying those points.

She had gotten it wrong.

"I am very disappointed," he said. "I had very high expectations for the both of you, based on your papers and work at the University of Maradaine. Some of the work you have done here has been extraordinary. Which is, frankly, the only reason you aren't both packing your bags yet. However, I might still decide that is necessary."

"Sir—"

"Promise me," he said, shoving an accusing finger at her. "Promise me that you will not further pursue this or any other constabulary matter, nor will Mister Golmin."

"I can hardly promise on his behalf," she said.

"You can't be so foolish to think I do not see your dynamic," he said. "If you tell him to not pursue it, he won't. He is ensorcelled by you. I am not. Promise me, or you will both be gone, and I will make a public disgrace of you both throughout the academic community. I will write to every one of the Elevens, every other High College of Maradaine, The Imperial College of Vedix, the Mocassan Conservatory of Knowledge, The Symposium of Rek Nayim, The Lyranan Bureau of Learning, every other place I can think of. I will ensure that you and Mister Golmin will be completely ousted from every single corner you could scurry to. You won't even be able to teach children in a shepherd village how to form their letters. Am I clear?"

"As glass, professor," she said, her voice trembling with fear. "We won't pursue it further."

THE LIST of supplies they had been set to get was extensive. Kennick was right, they would have to do quite a bit to get it all, because some of them were quite bulky. Kennick tore the list in half and handed it to Phadre when they arrived back at the house, telling the carriage not to wait for them.

"Get your things, and we'll load up in the mulecart and bring that back. We'd never get everything in the carriage."

"I don't know if you're right about that," Phadre said.

"I don't know if you're right about that," Kennick said in a mocking tone. "We're going to do it my way, because you and that slan of yours almost ruined everything. I don't care what brilliant concepts you have about magic and stars, Golmin. You're a rutting idiot who clearly thinks too much with his pisswhistle and lets that woman run you."

"That is not an accurate assessment," Phadre said. "And I advise you not to speak further disparagement of her."

"Or, what, you'll magic at me? That rutting slan—"

Phadre balled his fist and cracked Kennick straight in the nose. "Or you will yield to your betters."

Kennick held onto his face, blood gushing from his nose. "You're both crazy, you know that."

"Just get your part of the list and don't force me to do something truly damaging to you." Phadre went off toward the observatory, where most of the things he needed would be found.

Instead, he found Laslin, stripped to the waist, running around the device Jiarna had been concocting this morning.

"That seems right, but does it?" Laslin muttered. He banged on his head. "Remember! Remember! It's— no! It won't be safe. It isn't safe."

"Hey," Phadre said gently. "Everything all right, old boy?"

Laslin looked up at Phadre, eyes wild. "No! No, of course not. I had tried to build it, and then... and she tried, and she might have, but—"

"Easy, easy," Phadre said, holding up his hands calmly. "What can we do to help you?"

"Help me? No, no, nothing," Laslin said. "I'm fine. Not fine. Not safe, not— can you feel it? Like a buzzing fly in and out of the room that you can hear but never see and certainly never swat. But this can swat, if I can just—"

Laslin stopped and spun around so hard Phadre thought Laslin would injure his neck. He grabbed at his head and cried out, dropping to his knees.

"Hey, hey," Phadre said, coming to his side, grabbing the man's bony shoulders. "You're all right. You're fine. We just need to—"

"No!" Laslin shouted, jumping to his feet. "Nothing fine! Nothing safe! Have to hide!"

He ran down the stairs out of the observatory.

Phadre sighed. That poor man, what must be going on in that broken mind of his. He went through the observatory, gathering up the things he could from his list— a few spare crystals and tools, mostly, as at least one device he had planned to grab had been integrated into the contraption Jiarna had built. What was the point of that? He would need to ask her when a more opportune moment presented itself. He feared that one of those might be far off.

He came back down to the sitting room, to hear someone pounding on the door. He put down the supplies and answered it, finding Inspector Stendall there with a handful of officers behind him.

"Inspector," he said. "If you're here to berate me about the fiasco, well, I can't blame you. Jiarna is not yet here."

"Not exactly, Mister Golmin," he said. He looked through the notebook in his hand— the one Mister Orrickall usually had, and then pulled out a paper. "I have a Writ of Search here for these premises. Will you give no trouble while my men go about?"

"A Writ of— no, of course not."

"Is anyone else here?" Stendall asked.

"Kennick and Laslin are both about. But, I should say, Laslin, if you find him, he's not in a right state."

"Hmmm," Stendall said, signaling his men. Most of them came in, going about the house. "And you would know about not in a right state?"

"I'm hardly an expert, but this is plain to the layman," Phadre said. "What is this about?"

"Have you seen Mister Orrickall?"

"Not since he left the event earlier with his burned face," Phadre said.

"So, you didn't see him here at all?"

"No, I—"

"Specs!" one of the officers shouted from another room. Stendall raced off toward the voice, and Phadre followed, leading to the back library.

There on the floor was another body, another dried up husk like the others.

"Specs, it… it's him," the officer said. "It's Mister Orrickall."

"What?" Phadre asked. He was barely able to find his voice.

The response was the back of Inspector Stendall's fist against his cheek.

"How dare you?" he snarled. He held up the notebook. "He left me word to get a writ and come here, that he had a theory about the murderer. The mystical murderer. And that he was going to come check something. And I guess he found out."

"Found out what, how—" was all Phadre said before the officers all pulled him to the ground, and shackles went around his wrist, which hit him like ice.

Mage shackles.

"Phadre Golmin, consider yourself bound by law. The charges against you will include, but are not limited to, murder."

CHAPTER ELEVEN

THE DIAGNOSIS OF JIARNA'S ANKLE WAS exactly as Geordine had predicted, and some time could have been saved by merely allowing her to simply care for the injury in the first place. The doctor was easily persuaded from considering amputation, and he did provide a utilitarian crutch for Jiarna to use. She found it somewhat inefficient as well as unstylish, and on the ride home devoted a certain amount of her available brainpower— most was too focused on the pain— to ways to improve the crutch on both accounts.

That frame of thought collapsed when they reached Inchellian house and found it swarming with constables.

"What is this?" Professor Salarmin said as he got out of the carriage. Geordine helped Jiarna out as a pair of constables carried out what was obviously a dead body on a stretcher, covered in a cloth.

"No, no," Jiarna said, hobbling over to them. "Who is it? Who died?"

"Miss, you need to back off," the constable officer said, pushing his way past. His movement made the cloth shift, and she could clearly see the husk of a body. "No!"

"Jiarna," Geordine said sharply, grabbing her arm. "Steady."

"I can't be steady," she said. "Someone else is dead because I didn't—" Her heart dropped to the bottom of her body. It couldn't be. "Phadre!"

"Calm down," Geordine said. "I'm sure—"

No calm was possibly going to come. Reason had left her body completely. "Phadre!"

"Jiarna!" his voice came from inside the house.

He was alive. He wasn't the body. Then who—

Phadre came out, hands bound behind his back, led by Inspector Stendall.

"Professor, my apologies for the commotion, but we did come with a writ and—"

"What is going on?" Jiarna asked, limping over to them with Geordine dragged in tow. "I demand that you—"

"Miss Kay, keep your tongue," Professor Salarmin said. "But, Inspector, tell me what is about, and why you have my man here shackled. Who was that body?"

"The body was our examinarian, Mister Orrickall," Stendall said. "And he cracked this case, but at the cost of his own life. It's clear that the culprit of these 'mystical' murders was none other than Mister Golmin."

"That is absurd," Phadre said.

"Patently," Jiarna said. "We told you—"

"Yes, *you* told us," Stendall said sharply. He held up the notebook. "Orrickall figured it out. The first body on your caravan. The next one of your passengers. Then you happen to involve yourselves, claim that it wasn't magic, and destroy evidence."

"We did nothing of the sort," Jiarna said. "And it isn't magic, it's psionic—"

"It's all magic," Stendall said. "And this mage is the fellow behind it. And he killed Orrickall to try to protect himself."

Kennick came to the doorway, a bloody rag over his nose. "He's a rutting animal, he is! He attacked me as well!"

"I attest my innocence and demand council," Phadre said. "Jiarna, you know I did not—"

"I am certain you did not," she said. "Professor, stop this!"

"A dead body in my house, on top of everything else?" Professor Salarmin asked. "I don't know—"

"Sir, I swear—" Phadre said.

Salarmin held up a hand. "I will retain legal council for you, but— that will take a bit of time."

"And in the meantime, we're going to keep him locked in a cell with those mage shackles on, so he can't get anyone else," Stendall said. "And this one better not try to leave town."

"You suspect me?" Jiarna asked.

"At least in helping him cover his crimes," Stendall said. "We will—"

"She's not going anywhere," Salarmin said. "Right now, she can barely walk. We will be there with council in the morning."

Stendall nodded and dragged Phadre to the lockwagon. Jiarna's head was swimming; pain, confusion, anger, and a thousand other emotions pulled her mind every direction. She could barely even think, and as they pushed him inside, she shouted the only concrete thing she could put to words.

"I love you!"

"And I you!" Phadre called back. Then his face lit up. "Jiarna, I've got it! We have it in—"

That was all she heard before they slammed the lockwagon door on him, and rode off.

She wasn't sure how long she stood there on the house lawn, tears pouring out of her, and barely noticed when Geordine brought her inside the house.

"This is all a mess," Professor Salarmin said. "So many things to sort out. We need to get back to Lord Sweet's home. Poor Chren and Achariatt must be in a state."

"They must be?" Jiarna said. At this point she was on the couch in the sitting room, leg propped up on a pillow on the table. "I think they're the least traumatized of all of us right now."

"Miss Kay, if you could kindly just... not speak?" Salarmin said. "We still need to smooth things over with the Lord Sweet, though I think at this point repairs and additional devices are not the way to go."

"No," Geordine said. "Nothing is in a state where that makes sense."

"Right," Salarmin said. "Kennick, Geordi and I, we'll get back to the Lord Sweet's house, give a little show of pleasantries, make some apologies, Geordi will give her full charm to the Lord, since he likes her—"

"I'm not going to sleep with him," she said flatly.

"No, of course not," Professor Salarmin said. "But just... charm him."

She sighed and rolled her eyes.

"I can't go out there with my face like this," Kennick said. "I'm a mess."

"Yes, indeed," Salarmin said, looking the boy over.

If Phadre had done that to him, then he had surely done something to deserve it. And Phadre had done a very good job of it as well. "Quite unacceptable. Fine, you stay here, and… make a distillation of hastinite for the pain."

"It doesn't hurt that much," Kennick said.

"I meant for Jiarna," Salarmin said.

"Oh, of course," Kennick said. "Her pain."

"And I just sit here?" Jiarna asked. "I could—"

"You have done more than enough," Salarmin said. He came over and abruptly scooped her up in his arms. She instinctively grabbed his neck and held tight so she wouldn't tumble to the floor. "You will stay up in your room and not get into further trouble." He went for the stairs.

"Professor," she said, trying very hard to keep her voice rational and even. "My room is not a sensible place to install me. I can't navigate the stairs back down in my condition."

"I am quite aware of that, Miss Kay," he said as he went up the flight. "I think a bit of isolation, taking the night to think, would be very good for you. I think some dark times await you, Miss Kay. I may be getting a lawyer for Mister Golmin, but I doubt it will do much good."

"He is not the killer," she said firmly.

"I'm sure you believe that, and I imagine he is grateful to have your devotion, but the evidence seems quite compelling. I fear little will be possible to help him. Or you."

"I didn't—"

"Regardless," he said, going up the spiral to her room. "I don't know if you can count on the law to protect either of you. As I said, dark times await." He reached her room and placed her on her bed.

"You didn't even bring my crutch," she said. "And the water closet is downstairs."

He went to the steps. "You're very smart, Miss Kay, you'll work something out. Besides, Kennick will be here if you need anything."

He went down the steps— saints, those made a lot of noise, as did the steps down to the sitting room. She heard him say a few last words, and then he and Geordine left the house.

Jiarna was left with nothing but time to think.

Which was exactly what she needed to do.

***

JIARNA GAVE a brief consideration to the fact that she had promised the Professor that she would not pursue solving these murders any further, but that had been before Phadre had been arrested, so she rationalized that she was not solving the mystery so much as she was proving Phadre's innocence, and that was something she was morally obliged to do above any promise.

First steps were to minimize her pain and maximize her mobility. Kennick was supposedly preparing a distillation of hastinite, but she neither wished to wait for him to complete that task nor did she care for hastinite as pain relief. Clouded her thinking far too much to be useful at this moment. She needed to be sharp. She pulled herself up off the bed and inelegantly hopped over to her desk. She went through the drawers to find her bottle with the tincture she had developed for her bleeding days. It was effective at cutting pain and kept her head focused.

She normally took four drops on her worst days, so now she took eight.

In moments, she felt more relief and clarity than any distillation Kennick would make.

First step accomplished: pain managed. Next, mobility. She should have grabbed her crutch when the professor scooped her off the couch. Foolish error.

She did not have much in the way of tools or materials in her room. Not to make a crutch, at least. She did have a wooden desk chair, and with the knife and boltturner she had in her desk drawer, was able to disassemble it quickly. A little ingenuity with some belts, knickers and pillow down, she fashioned two chair legs into a makeshift peg that she could strap onto her knee. Ungainly, but workable to walk around for short periods without weight on her foot.

While working with her hands, she focused on the solution to the real problem.

The psychic killer had come here, to their home. Which meant that their action at Lord Sweet's estate had garnered the killer's attention, and that was a definite negative. But yet the killer had killed Mister Orrickall, which seemed incongruous. Perhaps because he had also been involved in the incidents at the manor, he was killed and brought here to frame Phadre.

Something wasn't sitting right about that.

Start at the beginning. Her thesis about the Cantons had proven wrong, so there was a fault in her reasoning. Work it through again.

First body, Mister Dreshin, on the 28th of Soran, outside the pension. Second body, Missus Grindel, 17th of Oscan, in an alley in the south Business District. Third, Underman. 4th of Poriman, in his shop. Fourth body, she never got the name of, Silver apple district, yesterday. Then Mister Orrickall, today, here in the house. That broke the pattern.

Pattern. Each of the others was nineteen days apart.

The night after Namali was full. Was that significant? Except today's broke the pattern. Why did it break the pattern?

Take it back again. Why was the killer doing these murders? What was the motivation? The regularity implied a need to be fulfilled. Perhaps as basic as eating.

Phadre had figured it out. What had he said? "We have it in—"

Inside? The killer had been inside the house. It was foolish to presume they weren't still inside the house.

As she tested her weight on her makeshift crutch, she heard Kennick coming up the stairs to deliver the distillation of hastinite, and suddenly the realization came to her. She knew what it was, and what Phadre was trying to say.

Which meant—

Kennick came up, and she quickly got in place so the bed was between them, weight on her good leg, knife and boltturner in her hands. Poor weapons, but what she had.

"I brought you the—"

"You stay back," she commanded. "Not another step closer."

"What?" he asked, stepping toward her.

"Back!" she said. "I know who you are. You're the killer."

"Jiarna, you must have truly lost your sense," he said. "How could I be the killer? They arrested Phadre."

"I figured it out, monster," she said. "We had it inverted."

"Inverted?" he asked. "You're talking nonsense. Take this for the pain and—"

"You killed Mister Dreshin, Missus Grindel,

Underman, the woman in the Silver Apple and Mister Orrickall," she said firmly. "And now you're here."

"I couldn't have done that, Jiarna," he said. "Come on. It wasn't like I was on the caravan with you all."

"Kennick wasn't," she said. "But *you*, the thing riding around in his skin right now, were."

The mirthless smile crossing Kennick's face confirmed her thesis.

CHAPTER TWELVE

"WELL, IT'S GOOD TO KNOW THE next mind I consume won't be an idiot," Kennick's mouth said. He held up the vial of hastinite. "This is just tea. I don't know how to make a distillation of hastinite, and neither did Kennick."

"What are you, exactly?"

"You tell me, Miss Kay," he said. "Since you surely have a theory."

"A psychic entity of some sort. No body of your own, instead feeding on new minds and jumping into their bodies. Which you have to do, because you fully consume each body you are in after nineteen days. Which meant each time we found a body, we were finding the perpetrator, not the victim. Why we heard a woman scream at the pension. You had jumped from Mister Dreshin into Missus Grindel."

He gave an appreciative shrug. "More or less accurate."

She kept her knife up, not sure what else she could do in the meantime. Part of her mind scrambled to come up with a plan. What could she do? A direct conflict would likely be fatal, either by whatever means of psychic attack it would use, or just by overpowering her. Kennick, for all his flaws, was stronger than she was. Running also seemed a poor choice. Those stairs were a challenge to traverse even in fit shape. With her current situation, she would not be able to get away from him, even with a solid distraction.

She did not yet have even the spark of an idea of how to distract him.

No plan at this point, save to keep talking, learn what she could, find a weakness. Satiate her curiosity.

"And Mister Orrickall," she said. "He had come to the Silver Apple district because we had detected you there. And you took him."

"Delicious," the creature in Kennick said. "He came upon me as the throes of my hunger set upon me. Which was really quite perfect, because his memory told me about these young, brilliant people who were on to me. And I remembered you both from the caravan. Sickeningly joyous, the both of you. Turns my stomach."

That was interesting. "So you can feel emotions."

"That's what I feed on, Miss Kay. Joy is rancid to me. But loneliness? Such a delicacy. Heartbreak? Divinity. And fear? Fear is the sweetest morsel of all." He stepped forward, and she instinctively stepped back. "Oh, and your fear is something I am going to savor."

That sent a chill through her spine, and made her stumble. Panic gripped her heart, which she cursed, since that was clearly what he wanted.

"Yes!" he cried. "Oh, you are marinating in it. I will feast so delightfully now! And then in your body, the things I will do to your beloved Phadre that will shatter his heart, making him such a ripe fruit to devour."

That flipped something in her, fear turned into rage. "I will never let you—"

"Anger," he said with a smile. "That's just spice to the banquet. I will—"

Whatever he was going to do, he didn't get a chance to say before Laslin charged up the stairs and pulled him to the ground.

"Run!" Laslin shouted, slamming wild punches into Kennick's face. "Get out!"

"Fool," Kennick said, grabbing Laslin's head. "I'll take you, then her!" For a moment, they both were engulfed in a yellow nimbus of energy that made every one of Jiarna's hairs stand up. She backed away further to the window. Nowhere for her to go.

She looked out the window.

The catwalk to the observatory.

A ridiculous, senseless thing to use in a normal situation, but this was not one of them. She unlatched the window and threw it open.

Both Laslin and Kennick screamed, the likes of which she had never heard before. Pain beyond imagining. Kennick's body started to wither, looking like all the other victims. But then he shrieked and let go of Laslin, dropping the disheveled man to the floor.

Laslin alive, breathing.

"Broken!" Kennick howled. "Useless! I can't get a grasp on your mind... and now..." He looked at his desiccated hands. "Now this body is useless, and the hunger is upon me." His dead eyes found Jiarna. "Thankfully I still have this meal."

Jiarna scrambled out the window and onto the catwalk. She went about a third of the way, on hands and knees, in a wild rush before she actually saw where she was, looking down to the ground dozens of feet below her.

Her pulse spiked, irrational panic gripping her heart. Pure emotion, nothing but fear, freezing her in place.

She was going to die.

Either the monster or the fall, she was going to die. That overwhelmed her mind so nothing else could get through, including making herself move another inch.

"Oh, you are saucing the goose, dear one," he said from the window. "It has been so long since I've had a meal like this!"

A beacon of rational thought burst through, a realization. *He can sense from a distance, but he needs physical contact to take you.* With that thought, she clawed her way up through the ocean of fear and forced herself to breathe.

"God damn it," she whispered to herself. "Jiarna Kay, you are going to move your hand. You are smarter than this. You can survive this."

And with that she moved her hand forward. Hands and knees, one foot at a time. Ignore the monster's taunts. Ignore the creaking of the catwalk, which was surely rotting and not going to hold her weight much longer. Irrelevant data. Not part of the set she needed to work with.

Move forward.

Solve the next problem.

Kennick's inhuman walking corpse climbed out onto the catwalk. The creaking became cracking. He took one step forward, and that crack became a horrifying snap, and Jiarna felt the whole thing buckle under her.

Faster. She lurched forward, reaching the observatory window as the one side of the catwalk snapped free and dropped, dangling uselessly in the wind. She glanced back to see that monstrosity in

Kennick's clothing still standing outside her bedroom window. He sneered and went back inside.

She climbed into the observatory.

JIARNA FIGURED, as she hobbled into the room on her makeshift peg, that she had, at best, three minutes for the monster to go down two flights of stairs, cross the house and climb up to the observatory. And she had no place to run to where she wouldn't meet him on that journey, and no way to lock him out.

"Blast and blazes!" she muttered, hoping a bit of angry profanity would stimulate her thinking. It was ridiculous that there was not a lockable door in here. The only thing here was—

—the psionic shield device she had been building this morning.

Saints, she had forgotten all about that. And she hadn't finished it.

Of course, it was just a matter of theory, based on Laslin's notes, with no real field test, but this was as good a time as any to do that. Maybe, if she could protect herself for long enough, the entity would burn out in Kennick's body. With no one to feed on, no victim to jump to, would it die?

She had no data with which to draw a conclusion. This was the field test, it would seem.

She knelt down within the circle of parts she had already assembled. A series of crystals that, when aligned within the charged magnetic ring— that was in place— should vibrate at frequencies that were disruptive to psionic energy, in lens boxes to focus that disruption. It should create an invisible wall around her that the creature— were it somehow pure, living psionic energy, as she had postulated— could not cross.

At least, if Laslin's theory had been correct. His own tests had broken his brain. But left him, apparently, immune to the creature's attack.

Would that be worth it? To lose her capacity to think, to be herself as she knew herself, if that was the price to live?

She didn't have time to ponder that. She just had to make it work. Have faith that she was correct.

"What an ironic thought," she muttered. She hurriedly put the last lens boxes in place. It would work. It would have to work.

All that remained was activating the magnetic ring with a galvanic charge, which she— hadn't built a means to create yet.

"Blazes," she muttered. It was too much to hope a timely bolt of lightning would crash through the ceiling at this moment. That was absurd. She needed—

She needed the galvanic crank that was on the floor.

And she had only built four lensboxes this morning, and there were now eight here already. In her panicked state, she hadn't even realized that. How?

Laslin, that beautiful, broken man. How much had he worked out?

"Please, Saint Deshar, let him be all right," she whispered, even though she wasn't usually one for prayer. This moment, though, it seemed appropriate. She got on the floor and hooked the crank's connections to the ring.

"Jiarna!" Kennick's dead, dry voice called. "I am so looking forward to this."

He wanted more fear from her.

She pushed the fear down by thinking through what she still had to do. Proper steps. Turn the crank, build up the charge high enough, close the circuit, magnet charged. Magnet activates the crystals, and that's the triple jack.

She turned the crank. Saints, that was harder than she thought it would be. She needed to do this sort of thing more often, build up arm strength. Still, she turned it, one rotation, two, three. The charge built inside, making the hairs on her arm stand up. The needle on the meter wobbled upward. Just a little more.

"Oh, I am going to delight living in your head, Jiarna," Kennick said, coming up the steps. "After I devour this delicious fear of yours. That will be so wondrous."

A few more cranks was all she needed. She kept turning, until the needle reached the top.

"And that fear, swirling with determination. Oh, my, very interesting. I wonder what this will taste like."

The crank was charged, all she had to do was close the circuit, and she'd be safe inside.

No, she thought. *You have it inverted.*

She stood up, turning to see the creature wearing Kennick's skeletal form. It walked slowly, perhaps out of necessity, perhaps to taunt her, but slowly nonetheless as it closed the distance to her.

"Oh, my," he said. "Such fierceness. Very noble, Jiarna." He came very close, as if he wanted to smell her before taking hold. "You are trying so hard. But I can feel it. I can taste it. Be honest, Jiarna. Under it all, aren't you afraid?"

He stepped into the circle with her.

"No," she said, stepping back. "I'm a scientist."

She slammed the peg foot onto the circuit switch, releasing the charge.

There was nothing to see, but she felt it like a

tetchbat that just missed her nose. With a hard, audible hum, the crystals vibrated.

The creature screamed.

Its fists pounded the air as if it were steel.

"What did you—" it howled. "I will swallow your soul! I will take such delight in consuming you! I will —" It raised a foot to smash one of the lensboxes, but it screamed again before it could get too close.

"Well," Jiarna said, letting herself collapse into a chair at the workdesk. She opened the lower drawer to find her hidden stash of celebratory Fuergan whiskey and cigarillos. Tonight she had definitely earned them both. "I hope you're in a talkative mood, monster. Because I would love to collect some data."

CHAPTER THIRTEEN

I T WAS WELL AFTER MIDNIGHT WHEN the Professor and the rest of the group returned, and Jiarna had indulged in perhaps one whiskey too many— she was in a room with a caged wolf, after all — but after what she endured, no one could fault her for that. It had left her in a state where she was a willing to wait for all of them to call out in concern first before she alerted them to where she was and what had happened.

Let them stew just a bit.

The entity had sat on the floor in its prison, utterly unwilling to share further information. This didn't surprise her, but it was a small disappointment. Here was something that was intelligent but not human. Or had it been at some point? Had this been some powerful telepath who had become like this? That was just one theory, she has quite a few, and while she did not have to solve that tonight, it was just one more piece in the grand puzzle of the whole universe that she would want to see completed.

"Jiarna!" Jovi called out. Based on what she could hear and see through the window, Jovi had come up to her room to check on her, and found only Laslin on the ground. "Where are you?"

"Observatory!" she called back. "Everyone get up here!"

The group—Professor Salarmin, Jovi, Acharriat and Geordine— came racing up the steps, stopping in a dead halt when they reached the top, staring at the trapped atrocity.

"What the rutting blazes is that?" Geordine asked.

"It— is that Kennick?" Acharriat asked.

"Miss Kay, explain!" Professor Salarmin said.

"That," she said, taking a puff on her third cigarillo of the night, "Is our psionic killer. I've trapped it. It kills by jumping from body to body."

Salarmin's entire expression changed. "Fascinating. Wait, I have it. It was in that examinarian, who was at the event, and that triggered the psychic compass— it does work!"

"It does," Jiarna said.

"It works!" Jovi shouted.

"And he came here and took Kennick, leaving the examinarian's body," Salarmin said. "But why?"

"He's not being very talkative," Jiarna said. "But I think the plan was to maybe kill and take over me and frame Phadre. But he had to settle for Kennick."

"Wait, is Kennick dead?" Geordine asked.

"Rather," Jiarna said. "Only that remains."

"That's a shame," Professor Salarmin said in a tone that indicated he wasn't particularly engaged in that aspect of the situation. "What an opportunity this is for research."

Jovi knelt down to look at the ring of lensboxes. "This is quite ingenious. How did you—"

"Laslin," Jiarna said. "Is he all right? The creature attacked him but somehow… couldn't."

"I'll check on him," Acharriat said, heading downstairs.

"Are you all right?" Jovi asked.

"I'm physically fine. Well, as fine as I had been last you saw me. I don't trust myself to descend the stairs safely, to be honest. Emotionally I am…" she paused for a moment. "Unable to properly diagnose at this time."

"Ingenious," Salarmin said, examining the devices trapping the creature. "We'll have to build something more proper here to encase it—"

"Presuming it survives," Jiarna said. "It does need to eat."

"Eat?" Jovi asked with a bit of a high pitch.

"Minds, emotions. It usually lasts nineteen days— the cycle of Namali, I need to figure out what that's about— but it might have spent itself and won't last that long."

It spoke. "I survived for decades when my host body was trapped in a collapsed mine, the ravening hunger driving me mad. I will escape this and consume you all."

"Well, that's not sporting," Salarmin said. "That galvanic charge should last, what, four days?"

"Four days, ten hours," Jiarna said, handing him a paper off the desk. "Though I have had a fair amount of whiskey so someone should go over my math. And someone should help me out of here and perhaps to my bed."

"Yes, yes," Salarmin said. "Jovi, be about that. Geordi, get to work with me here in crafting a more permanent encasement for the entity."

"I wasn't going to sleep anyway," Geordine said.

"Once you have Jiarna settled and Laslin— well, whatever could be done for Laslin— tell Acharriat to get to my lawyer and then the constabulary stationhouse. Get that inspector here with all haste, so we can liberate Mister Golmin."

That was the last thing Jiarna needed to hear, and with that, she let all primary awareness fall away. There had been some form of conversation with Jovi as she helped Jiarna down the steps, to the watercloset, and finally laid down on the couch in the sitting room— her bed was probably decided to be too much challenge to reach— but none of it registered in her memory. Her brain had just shut down completely, and for once, she was happy to let it.

A GENTLE KISS on Jiarna's forehead woke her from the deep, bone-weary sleep she hadn't remembered falling into.

"Where are you?" she mumbled, still half in her slumber.

"Right here with you, my love," Phadre's sweet voice whispered.

Memory flooded back, and she opened her eyes to see Phadre crouched next to her in the bright daylight.

"Phadre!" she shouted, throwing her arms around his neck and almost killing him with kisses. "I was— I thought— I didn't— and I—"

"I know," he said with a beautiful smile as she finished kissing him for the moment. "I've been fully briefed on everything that happened last night. Well, everything that other people could tell. The fallen catwalk out there tells me there's a fair amount of story I've not heard."

"I figured it out," she said. "And you were freed. That's all that matters."

"And you survived it," he said. "That matters quite a bit."

"I suppose it does," she said. Pieces from last night were still swirling in her head, finding places to lock in as permanent memories, fighting for relevance at the moment. "Laslin. Is he all right?"

"From what I've seen he's… Laslin? According to Acharriat, he was dead out, and then opened his eyes, sat up, and asked about cheese and mustard. Then he went down to the basement, like he used to. No worse than before, at least?"

"I wouldn't have made it without him," she said. "He was so brave."

"He's a good one," Phadre said. "I would have liked to have known him before."

"Same," she said. She sat up and made to get on her feet, before she remembered she still had part of her chair strapped to her knee.

"What is this about?" he asked.

"It was a makeshift solution," she said. "Much of last night was."

"And it worked," he said. "I've noticed your makeshift tends to be quite brilliant."

"Why, thank you," she said, steadying herself on her peg. Her crutch was here, and he took it up and presented it to her. "What is the plan now?"

"Well, we would have classes to teach today, though I've taken the liberty of cancelling them," Phadre said. "And we've now opened up a whole new avenue of research, which we should probably dive into."

"So, Professor Salarmin is not throwing either of us out of the house, off the team, or any of that?"

"What?" Professor Salarmin said as he came in, shirtsleeves rolled up to his elbows. Geordine was behind him, looking more than a little exhausted. "I mean, we're down a man, for one— I am quite saddened about Kennick— but there's too much going on for further disruption. It's a whole new world, and one where I need the dynamic brilliance of Kay and Golmin to help figure out. Further studies are needed, and I need—" He stopped, and stepped closer, taking her hand. "I am sorry, Miss Kay, for letting my conceit and anger blind me in these past days. You were right, and I promise to remember that when I feel challenged."

Jovi and Achariatt came in from the kitchen, both also looking more than a little haggard, a little shattered, but well. "Is that promise for all of us?" Jovi asked.

"Certainly," Salarmin said. He chuckled. "It doesn't hurt that this whole thing has already reached the ears of Lord Sweet and the other nobility of Yin Mara. They are very eager to pledge considerable sums to support us, including and especially Professor Associate Jiarna Kay."

A protected academic title. She presumed she'd have at least ten years before she received that, if at all. "That's quite the vindication," Jiarna said. "Though I might have to see what other offers I'm fielded."

"I will beat those offers," Salarmin said. "No matter what it takes. Though I expect you to start working on a proper paper. And more lectures. So much to do."

"And the ravenous psychic entity upstairs?" Jiarna asked.

"Well, your trap was very good, and Geordine and I have bolstered it, so I have very high confidence he isn't going anywhere for some time. And I'm famished. Are you famished? Phadre, you must be."

"Quite," he said. "Should I get started on lunch?"

"Nothing doing," Salarmin said. "To the Friendly

Hand and many sweet pigs! Come along, colleagues. We'll take the carriage to not strain Miss Kay's leg…" He was already out the door, and Geordine, Jovi and Acharriat went after him, each of them giving Jiarna a small nod of acknowledgment as they went.

"This means I outrank you," she said to Phadre as he helped her to the door.

"And deservedly so," he said. "But I'll get caught up in due time. I'm not going anywhere."

"Which is how I like it," she said, and she kissed him again, long and sweet, one of many kisses to come. If she had her way, they would never stop for as long as they lived.

Acknowledgments

So here we are with a very new adventure, on several levels. We have new characters in the center, we're outside of Maradaine, and we're publishing in a new way. All of this has been a journey, and I'm thrilled to share it with you.

That journey was shepherded by the work I've been doing on my podcast Worldbuilding for Masochists, and I can't express how much my co-hosts, Rowenna Miller and Cass Morris, are just the best people to work with. Brilliant, creative minds, and incredible anchors of support. More support came from patrons and fans, like Brian Yost, Nina Mulligan and Ember Randall.

Absolutely essential for this book was Britta Jensen, who helped midwife every aspect of this book. Very grateful for her counsel, advise, expertise and friendship.

Also instrumental were my usual sounding boards: Daniel Fawcett, forever my absolute rock when it comes to every element of this saga; and Miriam Robinson Gould, the best first reader I could ask for.

On top of that, my family remains a source of strength and inspiration. This includes my parents Nancy and Lou, and my mother-in-law Kateri. And, of course, my son Nicholas and wife Deidre, who have continued to put up with me during this incredible journey through Maradaine and beyond.

And thank you, dear reader. Because you have this book in your hands, you've joined me on this newest journey, and I'm so thrilled to have you with me.

ABOUT THE AUTHOR

Marshall Ryan Maresca is a fantasy and science-fiction writer, author of the Maradaine Saga: Four braided series set amid the bustling streets and crime-ridden districts of the exotic city called Maradaine, which includes The *Thorn of Dentonhill, A Murder of Mages, The Holver Alley Crew* and *The Way of the Shield*, as well as the dieselpunk fantasy, *The Velocity of Revolution*. He is also the co-host of the Hugo-nominated, Stabby-winning podcast **Worldbuilding for Masochists**, and has been a playwright, an actor, a delivery driver and an amateur chef. He lives in Austin, Texas with his family.